A Few Trivial Felonies

How many will these ladies commit?
And, they seem so . . . nice.

Sandra Sperling

A FEW TRIVIAL FELONIES

ISBN-978-0-9993683-1-2

Interior Formatting: Allusion Graphics, LLC/
Book Publishing, www.allusiongraphics.com
Cover by: Emily's World of Design

A Few Trivial Felonies

This is for Evelyn Nevala,
my favorite cousin and dear friend,
who is also a talented writer.
Her quick intelligence and
deliciously twisted sense of humor
add loads of pizzazz to my life!!!

Acknowledgements

I'm deeply grateful to my editor, Beth Bruno, who finds the weak transitions, confusing sentences, and holes in my plots, among other errors that are strewn through my manuscripts. The smooth-reading stories that result are greatly due to her touch. I couldn't do it without her!

Thanks to my husband, Dale, for choking down the edible parts of the occasional meal that gets left on the burner when I'm wrapped up in my writing. I especially appreciate his chiseling the charred remains of the above-mentioned meals from the pans.

Special thanks to my physical therapist, Lori Devins, whose treatments for vertigo and the endless patience she exhibited through weeks of therapy gave me back my life. At times, she likely wished she could use a whip and a chair to goad me along, but instead, she kept encouraging me to move forward with increasingly difficult exercises until I was back to normal.

About the Author

Sandra Sperling was born in Nevada and began her creative life in Minnesota, where, as a child, she wrote a play and a short story. Eventually she attempted a horror novel, but it didn't horrify. Her mother, while reading the manuscript, began to laugh helplessly and leaned against a door for support, sliding to the floor like a piece of cooked spaghetti. Deciding she was a failure as a writer, Sandy switched to painting drybrush watercolors. The pull to write, however, was too strong to resist, so while still in Minnesota, she again began to write, publishing some short stories and advancing to novels. She now lives in Kentucky with her husband. She enjoys taking nature walks, refinishing old furniture and reading.

Other Novels

The Beginner's Guide to Spouse Removal
Snowmelt

Chapter 1

DURING THE LAST WINTER that Rachel Christenson lived in northern Minnesota, she spent weeks shivering in an illegal outhouse. The region had suffered its normal low temperatures but received little snow, so despite six feet of soil covering the drain fields, they froze. By rationing toilet flushes, they managed, though the septic tank had to be pumped twice. Luckily, the sauna had a separate disposal system. Rachel fired it up twice a week, but throughout that miserable winter she always felt a little grubby.

Her husband, Nick, cobbled together a temporary outhouse from a cardboard and lathe freezer crate. He possessed neither a permit nor many carpentry skills, and he built the bench so high that when she sat on the icy platform, her feet dangled uncomfortably. She contracted an intestinal bug and suffered from the green-drizzling shits for an entire week, expressing her scathing opinions of the frigid region on the toilet walls with a red marker. She also scribbled down the daily high and low temperatures for San Francisco, Miami, Fort Worth, and Embarrass, Minnesota.

Nicholas wisely kept his mouth shut. But when he came down with the same flu bug, and, luckily for her, a more virulent and long-lasting strain, he said, “Maybe we *should* check out Texas this spring.”

“Fly or drive?”

“Fly. We can rent a car when we get down there.”

Despite his recovery from a series of small strokes that had plagued him late last summer, his blue-gray eyes had not regained their sparkle, he was far too thin, and he tired easily. He planned to retire at the end of March, when he’d have worked twenty-five years as an assistant manager at one of the remaining taconite mines.

• • •

Minnesota had a few patches of dingy snow left on the ground when they flew to Texas in April. It was warm and dry, and the real estate was marvelously cheap. But on the third evening of their trip, a tornado hit close to the restaurant where they were dining. It smashed their rented car and flattened the motel where they’d been staying.

“Are there many tornados in California?” Nick asked, while they sat at the airport with little more than the clothes on their backs, anxious to escape Texas.

“Um, I don’t think so. Not many thunderstorms either, at least not on the coast. But what about the earthquakes?”

“I think we’d be safe as long as we didn’t buy anything perched directly on top of a fault,” Nick said.

Rachel did the research. As much as she would have liked to live in the glorious sunshine of California, the land was far too expensive, especially considering that it wiggled as much as a two-year old sitting on a church pew. Also, climate change, drought, and fires were becoming increasingly prevalent. And after they'd spent their entire married life on one hundred wooded acres, they needed at *least* an acre to roam around on or they'd feel trapped.

• • •

Southern Oregon, near the coast, seemed as close to ideal as they could find. That it rained all winter was almost a treat compared to the six months of suffocating snow they usually struggled through in Minnesota. They flew out and fell in love with the clean, rugged area. They searched for a house with a view of the ocean or the mountains, or one with a pond or river on the property. They hoped to live on the outskirts of one of the small towns near the coast. And it had to be something that would cost about as much as the house they owned, although they *could* swing a small mortgage.

They found one on two acres of land. A stream trickled or roared through it, depending on the season, or so said the owner. The property included a guesthouse situated near the main house. They couldn't see the ocean, but Rachel comforted herself with the thought that this eliminated the tsunami hazard. If they cut down some trees in the front yard, they would have a reasonably good view of some mountains, but an even better view of a sagging, old mobile home parked directly across the road.

After visiting an attorney, they gave the owner an earnest payment and flew back to Minnesota to sell their house.

• • •

Their daughters, Barbara and Denise, were nineteen and twenty. Educated, working, and living with boyfriends, they were a bit discomfited that the house they'd always expected to inherit was no longer going to stay in the family. They *did* take full advantage of the furniture that Rachel no longer wanted and were willing to relieve her of even more, but she wasn't about to give either of them the antique dining set that she'd refinished or things she'd have to replace immediately.

She gladly left her job as a child-welfare counselor. Burned out from the endless stories of neglect and abuse, she refused to even think about a job in that field again. "What do you think about me not working?" she asked Nick. The idea of a future without the hassle of a job, at least for a while, appealed to her.

"Why not?" he said. "We have good investments, and my pension equals what many people earn on the job. Heating will be cheap. We also have inexpensive medical benefits until Medicare kicks in."

Rachel pondered this while she stacked some cartons of books she planned on hauling with them.

Nick added, "It'll give us the opportunity to do a little traveling too. After we get settled, that is."

He slurred his words a little. Rachel clutched the last carton of books and glanced at him in alarm, worried that he might be having another stroke. Relief filled her when she realized that his speech was impeded by the wad of fruity bubble gum he was gnawing on to replace the cigarettes he'd smoked for so many years.

• • •

By the end of July, their home sold for somewhat less than the house they were buying in Oregon. They stuffed the camper with their most cherished possessions, including their bed, which left enough room to sleep and brew morning coffee. They made good time, although the truck sucked down a lot of gas – enough to pay for a two-week luxury cruise in the Caribbean! The farther west they traveled, the healthier Nick looked, with pink in his cheeks and eyes bright with interest.

They spent the first night in South Dakota, so eager to reach Oregon that they decided not to make a side trip to explore the Black Hills. After their hot day on the road, Rachel insisted on stopping at a motel.

"I'm roasting. I won't be able sleep without air conditioning."

After two weary hours of searching for a motel with a vacancy, Nick pulled into the parking lot of a motel in Rapid City. Rachel dug out their pajamas, plus dried beef and bread for supper. "Grab some pop from that vending machine," she said to Nick. "We'll have a good breakfast tomorrow."

• • •

Although they got a late start, by pushing it a little, they made it to central Oregon the next day and spent the night in their camper. Shortly after noon, they turned into the driveway of their new home.

The sprawling ranch house seemed larger than Rachel remembered. Covered with white siding and lime-green trim, it blended well with the wooded landscape, although the lawn did need a good soaking. All was in order except the electricity, which *had not* been turned on as promised.

After they hauled the most vital items into the house, Rachel made a pot of green tea on the tiny stove in the camper. They walked around the yard, carrying honey-sweetened mugs of the mild brew and checking out the fruit trees.

"The former owner said he had four kinds of apple trees, plus peach and pear. I haven't the slightest idea which is which," Nick said.

"Your guess is as good as mine. Let's see if that greenhouse is salvageable. It'd be nice if we could grow our own salad makings year-round." She hoped a new interest would ease him into the transition of retirement.

The warped greenhouse door was slightly ajar, and Nick tugged and yanked to open it. They poked around, and Nick began to jerk dry weeds from the floor. When he yelped at discovering a small garter snake, Rachel flew out of the building. Her husband could deal with *that.*

A stone path led to a weathered bridge that crossed the nearly dried-up stream that ran along the side of their property. The bridge appeared to be sturdy enough, but she crossed it gingerly, ready to jump back if it started to creak, shudder, or sway. The path, which unmistakably led to the neighbor's house, was covered with flat rocks identical to theirs, except driftwood statues lined the path on their side. All the skillful carvings depicted the Virgin Mary. *The neighbors must be devout Catholics,* she thought.

Mature pines soared skyward on both properties. The trees, the silence, and the statues gave her a feeling of reverence. Uneasy, she wondered if she weren't inadvertently trespassing on the property of some religious order. Not wanting to make an enemy on her first day, she slipped back onto her own side of the bridge while rubbing her suddenly goose-pimpled arms.

Chapter 2

VIVIAN WOULD HAVE TAKEN back her maiden name after the divorce, but Skag was even worse than Snell, or so she thought. Besides, it made things easier that she and her son had the same last name. She stood at the spotted bathroom mirror and applied lavender shadow to her eyelids, followed by charcoal liner. She finished up with three coats of black mascara on her stubby lashes. Lastly, she doused herself with some pungent dollar-store musk. All this effort was made merely to stop at the grocery store, where her current prey was working. He wasn't particularly handsome, but he was clean, muscular and, most importantly, employed. Not ideal, but she had no choice; her generous child-support payments would cease in two years. She needed a husband, or at least a live-in boyfriend, to help pay for her mobile home.

"Dusty, come on into town with me," She yelled to her son from the dark-paneled kitchen, while she rubbed a tablespoon full of generic lotion into her battered hands. She needed a haircut as badly as her son, but she couldn't afford two.

He leaned out of his bedroom doorway, meeting her eyes, which were the same reddish brown as his. "Naw. I'm down-loading a new game."

Lately, if he wasn't on the computer, he was watching old Arnold Schwarzenegger movies.

"It can load without your help. You *have* to get a haircut before you go stay with your dad."

"I hate going to his house! His wife bitches about every crumb I drop on the tablecloth." He slouched, leaning against the wall, peering through his shoulder-length hair. "Besides, there's nothing to do in Fresno."

"That don't matter. It's only three weeks, and he always buys you a years' worth of clothes." She grabbed her keys and checkbook from the cluttered counter. "Come on, let's go."

Dusty followed her sullenly, locking the door behind him. They walked through the desiccated, treeless yard to an aging blue Taurus. Before they got in, a mid-sized moving van pulled into the driveway opposite them. The truck veered to the right behind a thicket of trees, effectively cutting it from view.

"I hope the new neighbors are livelier than the last batch," Vivian said. She turned the key and punched the gas pedal several times before the car would start. It took only minutes to reach the small strip mall in the little coastal town of Crusty Beach, where she dropped Dusty at thc barbershop with orders to have his hair cut short.

Reaching the grocery store, she raced through the aisles, snatching groceries until she reached the meat section. The new butcher—single and from exotic

Milwaukee—was at work marking prices on plastic cartons of liver. Vivian rubbed the inner corners of her eyes to remove eyeliner boogers, thrust forward her boobs, and approached the counter. She smiled brilliantly.

"What's good in sausage today?" She'd asked him versions of that question several times, but he never seemed to pick up on the fact that she wasn't necessarily talking about pork and beef.

"I've got some coarse-ground German wieners. It's my own recipe—good with sauerkraut. I eat them all the time." He stacked containers of liver five high and placed them on a stainless steel cart while they talked.

"I'll take a dozen." She watched as he wrapped the hefty wieners in a piece of freezer paper, taping them shut, hoping Dusty liked them. They were flesh-toned and so strongly resembled an uncircumcised penis that she wondered if she'd be able to gag them down. Still, she knew that butchers made a good living, so she grinned at him and said, "I do like them big." She fought the queasiness that crept over her.

He grinned back at her, exposing teeth that were strong and thick, like white dominoes. He weighed the wieners, marked the price on the package, and went right back to the liver. She sped away, wondering how she could get him interested enough to visit her while Dusty was away. There wasn't time to work on him today, because she couldn't be late for her job at the Crusty Beach Restaurant, where she worked as a cook. She dashed to the check-out line and then lugged the bags out herself, relieved to see that Dusty was already in the car, freshly barbered from his yearly haircut and looking disconcertingly mature.

When they got home, he ran into his bedroom, no doubt to work on the computer. Vivian put the groceries away and plopped three of the enormous wieners into a saucepan to boil, hoping they'd darken when they cooked so they'd look more palatable. She sped to her bedroom, slipped into her work uniform, and tied on an apron, after which she set the table and heated a can of beans. The wieners hadn't changed color, unfortunately, so she drained the water from the pan and plunked it on the table.

"Lunch is ready," she called.

Dusty served himself some beans, then speared one of the spicy-smelling wieners and put it on his plate. He stared at it, looking a bit pale.

Vivian put one on her plate, more than a little hesitant to eat it. It looked so remarkably human she was tempted to call the cops. Instead, she grabbed steak knives from the drawer and sliced off the uncircumcised tip of the wiener, stabbed it with her fork, and smeared it with ketchup. She popped it into her mouth and chewed; a drizzle of greasy ketchup ran from the corner of her mouth.

Dusty stared at her, his eyes bulging in horror. His pallor became greenish and he stumbled to the kitchen sink and barfed.

Vivian swallowed the bite she was chewing, but her appetite was gone. The wieners were enough to turn a cannibal into a vegetarian. She dropped the butcher from her short list of eligible men while she drove to work. But where could she find someone to replace him? And how could she disguise those wieners to make them edible?

Chapter 3

RACHEL'S NEW HOME IN Crusty Beach had more space than the Cape Cod house in Minnesota. Because it was all on one floor, it seemed vast. She'd pushed for it, not because she particularly liked it, but if Nick should end up in a wheelchair, the open floor plan would allow him access to nearly every room.

He had just turned 47, young for a stroke, but his blood pressure had risen sharply and unexpectedly, causing a small blood vessel in his brain to rupture. Medication had returned his pressure to normal, increasing his life span to possibly thirty years or more, but one never can tell.

The front entry hall led back to the casual family room, which featured a fireplace and a screened-in porch on the west. To the right were a formal living room and two spare bedrooms, devoid of furniture. Looking at them made Rachel regret having been so generous with her daughters. Directly to the left of the entry was the dining room, where they ate most of their meals, mostly canned though they'd been for the past few days.

The house came with a sizeable breakfast nook, which Rachel commandeered. She set up her computer on a pair of packing cartons. The bright room had windows facing south and west, bringing in lots of natural sunlight. She'd discovered that when the wind blew the branches just so she had a glimpse of the ocean, something she kept to herself. After they got settled, she'd do some judicious thinning of the tall pines that grew on the western slope of their property.

After arranging the furniture they *did* have, the all-white rooms somehow looked even more barren.

Nick said, "We really can't afford to buy anything more until we get the mortgage paid off."

"Three years. Damn! We'll have to go to some garage sales. I *must* have a table or desk for my computer, and you need a couple of stools for the greenhouse. And that's just for starters."

She slid a casserole of dehydrated potatoes with cheese sauce into the oven and dumped the last can of green beans into a saucepan. "We have to go to the grocery store today; I'm out of meat and milk. And coffee. Maybe they'll have some ads posted."

"We'll go right after we eat. What day is it anyway?"

"I have no idea."

"I'll catch it on the truck radio." He sauntered through the breezeway into the garage to listen, having left their widescreen television in Minnesota, afraid it would break en route. They hadn't found the smaller one yet or either of the radios packed in the numerous boxes stacked in the garage.

Rachel set the table, then sank down, cradling her cheeks in her hands. She needed a nap. All the excitement of the move was melting away, being replaced by exhaustion. She shuffled to the counter and poured herself the last cup of coffee. Left over from breakfast, it was thick and bitter, but she grimaced and swallowed it down, needing a lift to get through the rest of the morning. Tonight she'd go to bed early and catch up on her sleep.

Nick came into the kitchen. "It's Wednesday. And before we buy groceries, let's go down to the beach. We've been here for five days and we still haven't been to the ocean." The sparkle was back in his eyes.

Her exhaustion melted away. "Yes!" She pulled the potatoes from the oven and shoved a spoon into them. "Eat fast," she ordered, filling their plates.

• • •

Climbing down to the ecru-colored sandy beach opened up an entirely different world to Rachel. The waves were small, but they pushed shallow sheets of water high up on the beach. The day was warm and sunny, so she took her shoes off and stepped into the water. She shrieked and jumped back onto the dry sand. "That's as cold as Lake Vermilion in May! Geez!"

Nick laughed at her, his cheeks pink. "Well, you're used to that. Go ahead! Take a quick dip."

"No way in hell!"

Two boys, about ten-years old, were wrestling a large piece of driftwood up some steps on the steep bank, and Nick helped them with it. They came back down together.

"What are you going to do with that driftwood?" Rachel asked.

"A lady buys it from us. Her husband carves on it." The boy wiped his hands on his jeans.

Maybe that's where the Virgin carvings on the bridge path came from, Rachel thought.

"What's this I hear about sneaker waves?" Nick asked.

The taller boy, a blonde wearing a red and white striped T-shirt answered, "They're huge waves that come in out of the blue and suck you out to sea. Never turn your back on the ocean." He sounded like a wise old sea captain from two centuries ago.

Rachel asked, "When do they usually come?"

"Anytime. They sneak up and snatch you, and once they hook their claws into you, there's no escape." He spoke solemnly, his eyes darting to the water.

"And don't stand on logs on the beach," said the shorter, brown-haired boy. "A wave can come up and flip the log over onto you. You're trapped, then crushed and drowned. It's an agonizing way to die." His pale green eyes bulged as he attempted to convey the seriousness of the danger.

"Make sure you listen to your radio for tsunami warnings. You don't ever want to be stuck down here when the tide comes in, either."

"Yeah, you'll be dragged out into the ocean."

She had read about coastal living and knew what the boys said was true, but she found their version as ominous and horrifying as something Dean Koontz could have written. The boys went south, and Nick and Rachel headed north. She continually scanned the watery horizon for danger.

"I wonder if I shouldn't try my hand at some driftwood carving," Nick said. "Did you bring that set of chisels?"

"Yes, they're in one of those boxes in the garage." His former venture into carving had produced a set of decorative, tole-painted spoons with warped handles. A true labor of love and early poverty, she'd left them in Minnesota at the landfill, along with warped ceramic ashtrays and some of the art produced by the girls in grammar school.

The ocean remained calm while they walked, with no deadly waves attacking. It had a peculiar scent that Rachel struggled to identify but couldn't. It most certainly didn't resemble any of the household products claiming to smell like a fresh ocean breeze, at least none that she'd ever used.

Far up on the beach a man with a black dog waved at them, but they only waved back and left, not knowing how long the supermarket in Crusty Beach stayed open. The small town was named after Roger Crust, who'd opened a trading post there in the 1800s. The town sported a dozen stores and businesses, enough to supply their daily needs, along with a variety of shops that opened seasonally to cater to the tourists.

• • •

Back in the truck after they were done shopping, Nick said, "I copied ads for a few rummage sales near here.

Maybe we'll find some furniture and meet some of the locals."

Rachel pushed her ash-blonde, chin-length hair behind her ears. "I want to be a little more settled before we start having guests." He'd *always* craved socializing more than she had.

"Well, I miss seeing friends."

"Invite some local guys. Just for you, at first."

He frowned and sighed audibly, but said nothing.

Different region, same conflict.

Chapter 4

NOBODY KNEW WHAT AILED Har Lundahl. He'd neither spoken nor written a word since he'd been rescued from a POW camp in Vietnam decades ago. Physically, the man was in good shape and looked considerably younger than he was. Because he kept himself clean, ate whatever was put in front of him, and never complained about anything, Ruth didn't mind his silent presence. He spent his days carving the Madonna from driftwood and his evenings sharpening his chisels, never bothering a soul.

Ruth almost wished he would. She worked at a hobby shop in Crusty Beach one or two days a week, cutting mats and framing photos, watercolors, and assorted artwork, and she saw a few people there. But working in the back room, her contacts were short and usually involved only business, such as selecting mat colors and styles of frames with her customers.

The exceptions were brief but interesting conversations with her boss's nephew, Ben Larkin, who drove up from Eureka every couple of months to visit his aunt and uncle. She felt oddly protective of him, since he had an aura of gentle sadness about him, often reaching out his hand as if to touch the back of someone who wasn't there. In the two years she'd lived here, Ruth hadn't joined any organizations where she could meet people, but she didn't want to spend another endlessly rainy winter listening only to Har's knees creak when he hobbled to and from the garage workshop. But better that than getting stuck with a bore, or worse still a gossip who tried to pry information out of her.

She stirred the chunky vegetable soup she was making for lunch and tasted it, then added a teaspoon of allspice. While waiting for it to come to a boil, she wiped smudges off the pale aqua walls and adjusted the bottom half of the aqua and white checkered café curtains on the two windows. She pushed all the chairs in at the square oak table. The soup began to boil, so she turned the heat down and covered the pan.

Someone knocked on the front door, startling her. She left the spacious country kitchen, hurrying to the adjacent entry hall. She unlatched the screen door and opened it but didn't step back from the woman who stood there, even though she appeared to be harmless. "Yes?"

"I'm Rachel Christenson, your new neighbor. I came to ask you about a driftwood carving placed by my front door last night. It looks much like those on your bridge path."

Her hair was dark blonde and shining with health. She had a friendly, though puzzled expression on her face. Seeing her, Ruth was glad that she'd recently applied the pale, not quite platinum color to mask her white hair. "Oh ... Har would have put it there. He carves them all the time. Consider it a gift."

"Well, thank you. We're not Catholic, but the carving is beautifully done. I'd love to keep it."

Laughing, Ruth answered, "We're not Catholic either. It's a mystery why he carves the Virgin. She's the only thing he *does* carve. And, my name is Ruth Lundahl." She liked the woman and considered inviting her in, but when it came to people, especially those living right next door, keeping up an emotional barrier was always wise. As starved for friendship as she was, she had to be wary.

"Thank him for me. By the way, your soup smells wonderful. I put allspice in mine too." She grinned, stepped back from the door, and left.

Ruth watched her walk away, noting her slim figure, broken by hips just a little too wide. The woman had either come from or spent considerable time on the Iron Range. Her dialect was unmistakable, causing homesickness to pulse through Ruth. Sadly though, she'd have to clear up some of the problems in her life before she dared make a friend.

She returned to the kitchen and set the table with bowls, adding a platter piled with crackers, cheese, and packaged ham. The side door of the garage banged shut, the porch door on the back of the house squealed open, and Har walked in. Creak, thud thud, creak, thud thud, creak, thud thud, until he reached the kitchen. Ruth placed the soup on the table and ladled it into their bowls. The sounds of quiet chewing were the only noises. They ate quickly and Har went back to the garage, taking an earthenware mug of coffee with him, leaving Ruth to clean up the few dishes.

Ruth sighed, the weight of lonely depression threatening to crush her. Lately it seemed as if the caffeine of her life was gone for good, leaving only pale, perked-out grounds for her to subsist on.

Chapter 5

RACHEL WALKED AWAY FROM Ruth Lundahl's house and thought that she'd do well to look for a friend elsewhere. While not exactly unfriendly, the woman had shown no desire to become better acquainted.

Through the trees that lined the driveway, she caught sight of a woman getting her mail from the middle box. She wore a snug orange tank top and butt-hugging teal blue slacks. Her long, rust-colored hair was tied back with a chartreuse scarf. Rachel slid behind a tree, waiting until the woman crossed the road and disappeared back into her mobile home before she edged back onto the driveway, glad that she'd worn her navy-blue hooded sweatshirt rather than her highly visible red one. The woman might possess a perfectly fine personality, but her taste in colors would be difficult to face over midmorning coffee. She wasn't quite desperate enough to become friendly with that neighbor, but she wanted to keep her options open. The time would soon come when she wanted to talk with someone besides Nick.

She opened her mailbox and removed a lone bill; the junk mail hadn't yet caught up with them. Nick had washed the flat black box and replaced the previous owner's name with small, stick-on letters saying *Christenson.* It needed no other maintenance. Such simplicity was *so* Nick: exactly what was needed and not a particle more.

The Lundahls had painted their name in black on the side of their aluminum box. The flag was faded red, but the cover fit tightly, and the post was a carved piece of driftwood featuring the Virgin with secretive, downcast eyes. Like Ruth, she gave none of her feelings away.

Vivian Snell had hurriedly lettered her box in magenta and painted the flag the same color. The door was twisted and hung from one hinge like a tongue attached by a shred of skin; it would never again shut. Duct tape held the box to its platform, and an artificial clematis vine coiled up the tilted post. Rachel cringed and debated whether or not she should become acquainted with Ms. Snell, but curiosity won out. She'd go there some day soon, because she simply *itched* for a peek at the interior of her trailer.

She ripped open the bill while she strode across the dry lawn to their house. *We need some of that famous Oregon rain*, she thought. The grass was beginning to brown, despite Nick's daily watering from the creek. He used the pump and sprinkler system left by the former owner, which worked only moderately well due to the low water level in the creek. Luckily, the temperatures had stayed in the sixties, keeping the fire danger low.

The garage door stood wide open, and Nick was organizing the space in the rear of the deep garage. The three-stall building was fully equipped with cabinets and a solid workbench. "I found my chisels," he said. "But the pruning shears and other garden tools were obviously left in Minnesota."

"Let's drive into town to see what they carry at that hardware store," Rachel said.

"Better wait till I get the next pension check, or I'll have to dip into savings, and I don't want that."

"We'll dip into mine. Let's go to some of those garage sales too. I'm desperate for a table in the breakfast nook. And I could really use a sewing machine," she said. "I wish I hadn't given so much stuff to the girls!"

"How many sales are there today?"

"Four. All within eight miles."

"Okay. I could use a break," said Nick, wiping his brow with the back of his hand. "Let's go!"

• • •

At the first sale, Rachel found an old table with a white metal top and chrome legs that the owners were selling for only eight dollars. It had built-in leaves that pulled out, doubling its size. At the same sale, Nick came across a small, electric chainsaw that was almost new. At another, he found seed flats and pots and bought them all. He didn't run across any stools to use in the greenhouse, but the rummage sale season would last a long time in this climate.

At the last sale, Rachel found a vintage portable Singer. It only sewed a straight stitch, but since she planned to use it mostly for making curtains and replacing zippers, it would do the trick. It came with several bobbins, some extra attachments, and even a package of needles. Fortunately, the machine still had its instruction booklet. The paint wasn't worn from the platform of the machine, so it hadn't been used very much, and she got it for a song.

• • •

After the house was organized, Nick began to search the beaches for driftwood to carve his trolls. Rachel accompanied him a few times, but more often stayed home, reveling in her precious time alone.

She'd secretly checked out the trees that blocked her view of the Pacific and discovered they weren't located on their property, but on the acreage downhill from theirs. The owner was unknown, but he or she hadn't built a house on the steep and rugged terrain. Because the trees were so huge, cutting them down was out of the question. Each would take her a week with an ax or saw, and she didn't have nearly enough extension cords to use Nick's chainsaw. Besides, fresh saw and ax marks would look suspiciously unnatural on the stumps.

Instead, Rachel pruned the branches off, but not by climbing the trees. Whenever Nick was gone, she opened a window in her breakfast nook and removed the screen. Then, perched on a chair, she sniped away at the branches, using an old Remington rifle that had belonged to her grandfather. The first time she'd shot the heavy rifle in the house, her ears had rung for hours, so she invested in some earplugs. She never shot more than three times, not knowing how far the 30-30 could be heard. Already, she'd managed to rid some trees of several branches, opening up a small but constant view of the ocean. With what they'd paid for the house, she figured she was entitled.

One day, right after shooting off another branch, she went outside and began to water the bed of perennials in the front yard when a police car drove in. A young, rather scrawny officer got out.

"I hope you don't have bad news," she said. Her heart speeded up at the thought of Nick being in a car accident.

"No, only some questions."

She turned the hose down to a mere trickle and placed it in the center of the flower bed.

After writing down her name and where she had lived before, he asked, "Did your husband bring any firearms with him from Minnesota?"

Oh, shit. "No," she said, with a smile. "He doesn't hunt and never owned any." It was the literal truth, and the police officer perceived that she was telling it. She willed him not to catch the scent of gunpowder that clung to her like dollar-store perfume.

"Have you heard anyone shooting around here lately?"

"Um, come to think of it, yes. A couple of times. The shots came from that direction." She pointed to the far left of Vivian's trailer. Needing something to busy her hands, she rubbed her sore right elbow, which she'd injured in a minor bicycle accident.

He jotted down the information in a small notebook, then welcomed her to the community at great length.

Rachel drew a deep breath of relief when he finally drove away. If she was careful about the times she did her *pruning*, she'd be able to continue. It might be better, though, to shoot during the rainy season, when people were inside and less likely to hear it.

She chuckled, wondering why it never dawned on that cop to ask if *she* had any firearms. He'd evidently never encountered any Minnesota women. Just for the hell of it, she went into the breakfast nook and shot off one more branch.

Chapter 6

ON THE SAME EVENING that Vivian drove back home from dropping Dusty off in Fresno, she dyed her hair rhubarb red. She'd taken one vacation week, gambling that it would be enough time to bag an eligible male. Since she'd been unable to ferret out any men in Crusty Beach, she planned to spend the entire week hunting for guys at festivals and bars up and down the coast.

But not tonight. As much as she hated wasting time, she was tired and had dark pouches of exhaustion beneath her eyes. If she felt like this at thirty-eight, how would she feel in five years? And by then, a good night's sleep probably wouldn't get rid of the bags, so she'd better find a man soon. This week if possible. She made an almost adequate income as a cook, but lately her legs *ached* by the end of her shift and she'd developed a few spider veins. If she took after her mom,varicose veins were right around the corner. She simply had to snag a man before she had those horrid-looking things to contend with. But with her wrinkles, which seemed to get deeper by the week, it wasn't going to be easy.

She tore her clothes off and threw them on the floor, then stepped into the dinky tub to take a fast shower. Afterwards she squeezed vitamin E from capsules and mixed it with generic hand lotion, which she smeared over her face and body. The sticky concoction would stain her threadbare sheets, but enough of it would soak into her skin to smooth it out. In the morning, she'd scrub it off with a loofah and apricot hulls, and her skin, what was left of it, would glow and look good for days.

Vivian went to the dark-paneled kitchen and made a peanut butter sandwich, swallowing it down while in the nude and shivering all the while. The trailer felt damp and chilly, so she turned up the thermostat and let the furnace run for one cycle. She tugged an oversized T-shirt over her head. Finally, she pulled down the ratty, spare quilt from her closet shelf and spread it on top of her thin blankets. If she could stay warm, she'd be able to sleep until late morning, which was the most effective beauty treatment she'd ever discovered, except for getting laid. And, it was a lot safer.

• • •

Vivian dressed in flame orange to attract attention and left before nine the next morning, driving up the coast to an art festival in Newport. Giddy with anticipation, she decided that she'd flirt with *any* man who was both single and still breathing, her only stipulations. Surely, she'd be able to bag at least one man in a week.

She parked, refreshed her musk perfume, and began to roam slowly around the grounds, pasting a pleasant look on her face while she scanned the crowd. Most of the men were with women, but she finally spied a lone male examining paintings under an awning. She wandered around the display, attempting to look fascinated by the watercolors of the ocean, which interested her not at all. The man had gray hair, but it was thick and he was reasonably thin. He was dressed in jeans and a polo shirt, but something about them looked expensive. Good enough. She pivoted and casually swung her hand into his crotch.

"Oh! I'm so sorry! I was so mes ... mesmerized by the art that I didn't see you." She smiled, attempting to look apologetic, wistful, and innocent, while shooting her gaze straight into his eyes.

He grimaced. "Apology accepted." He escaped to another painting.

Although he'd been dismissive, she followed him, saying, "I wisht I could paint."

"Why don't you?"

"My only talent is cooking." That should catch his interest; most men hated to cook. He moved to the next wave painting, a mauve one with pink froth.

"My fiancée is into that too. She specializes in French cuisine."

"Oh, lucky you." *Well, lah-di-dah.* Vivian remained behind while the man went to the next painting, pretending to be intrigued by the pink and purple wave. After he left the booth, she waited a minute, then departed, strolling in the opposite direction and away from him.

Vivian next hit on a dude who carved statues of curvaceous women with a chainsaw. She slinked away in embarrassment when he quietly informed her he was gay, but she had a suspicion he'd said it only to be rid of her.

In the tent where beer was being served, she downed two tall mugs before she was relaxed enough to look around. She instantly felt out of place because she was the only woman there. The men leered at her as if they'd pegged her as a hooker, which wasn't all that distant from the truth. Irritated, she clumped out and stomped to the beach to clear her muddled head before starting home.

Noticing a pair of men far down the beach, Vivian stuffed a piece of gum into her mouth and moved toward them, swaying her hips provocatively. When she reached them, she dropped the sway and passed right by, since they were clearly pensioners and had been for a considerable time. Although she hadn't stipulated age in her list of criteria, these two were decades older than she was interested in. After about five more minutes of plodding along the beach, she wearily turned around, giving up her manhunt for the day.

• • •

The next day, before heading out to Reedsport, she walked to her mailbox to collect the mail, where she met her new neighbor. The woman was about her age, but somewhat thinner. Her hands looked unused, virginal.

The newcomer smiled and said, "Hi, I'm Rachel Christenson. My husband and I took early retirement and moved here from Minnesota. And you are ..."

"Vivian Snell. I work at the Crusty Beach Cafe as a cook." She quickly glanced through her many bills and looked up. "My teenage son is usually here—he does odd jobs for people—so if you need something done, ask him. Anyways, he's visiting his dad for three weeks at the moment."

"I'll remember that. And once we get settled in, maybe you'd like to come over for coffee."

"Yes, I'd like that," Vivian said, while thinking, *Just what I need, a spoiled brat of a woman in my life.* She winced when she thought of Rachel seeing the filthy orange carpeting and the stained furniture that filled her living room. She really should clean it, but then she wouldn't have time to track down a man, and Vivian did have her priorities in order. "Yes," she repeated, glancing at her watch. "I gotta go. Nice meeting you." She hurried to her house, wondering what Rachel had done to deserve a fancy house and a husband with money. *It ain't fair.*

The rest of her vacation was just as hopeless, with no men showing any interest in her. She drove all the way to Medford and slept in her car. She hit five bars, but only found men who wanted one-nighters. Maybe she'd developed the look of desperation that so many single women acquired. Her best friend at the restaurant had eventually settled for an old fart thirty years her elder, just so she could adequately feed, clothe, and buy disposable diapers for her pre-school children, whose father had taken off shortly after the birth of the third one.

Vivian wasn't quite that hopeless yet, but it wouldn't be long before pensioners slipped onto her radarscope.

Chapter 7

DURING THE FIRST WEEK of September, Ruth worked at a craft store every day, filling in for the owner, whose husband had required emergency surgery. Business was slow, since people had already stocked up for school, and it was too early for them to purchase hobby supplies to ease them through the rainy months. After she'd given the store a thorough cleaning, she spent her time reading and was immersed in a mystery when Rachel walked in.

"Hi! I need some high-quality paper for my printer," she said, standing by the door. "Do you carry it, or will I have to drive to Medford?"

Ruth smiled and pointed to the rear left corner of the room. "Over there, and it's on sale. But we no longer keep much ink in stock; you'll probably have to order it."

Rachel dumped three reams onto the counter and looked around the store, expressing surprise at the variety of craft supplies, easily as much as a large city shop would carry.

Ruth guessed her thoughts. "People around here need pursuits for the rainy months. I hook rugs."

"Oh. I used to sew a lot when my kids were little, but then I got a job and didn't do much of that for fifteen years. I plan on taking it up again." She ran her fingers along the packages of paper, then asked, "Is it *really* that bad? The rainy season, I mean."

"Well, it's warm enough to be outside, but you usually need an umbrella and can't do much of anything unless it's with one hand." She rang up the merchandise and took a check from Rachel. "After the storms, some people go beachcombing for driftwood and glass floats. It's usually too nippy for me." She placed the paper into a plastic bag, careful not to smash the corners.

"My husband used to carve a little," Rachel said. "And he's started doing some trolls on driftwood, so he's all set up. Maybe he could visit your husband. At least they'd have something in common."

Ruth sighed. "Ah ... my husband had a stroke and can't speak. Company really rattles him. Even mine bothers him at times." She rubbed the fisted knuckles of one hand onto the palm of the other.

"Oh, I'm sorry to hear that. My husband had three mini strokes last year, which is why he retired. He has a little numbness on his tongue, but that's all."

They evaluated each other silently, and Ruth began to open up a little, something she'd rarely allowed herself since moving here. "We're from Minnesota, on the outskirts of Hibbing. You sound like you're from the Range too."

"Yes, we lived outside of Ely. Now I know why I feel drawn to you; it's the familiar accent."

Ruth would have liked to have a longer conversation, but a customer came in dragging three noisy children, and Rachel left.

Her last customer of the day was Ben Larkin, who caught her just as she was about to lock up. As usual, he wore tan chinos and a safari jacket in a darker shade, which nearly matched his brown hair.

"I just need a couple of old-fashioned steno pads. I drove up from Eureka after my last class and forgot mine. I came to help Aunt Martha."

"That's good of you."

"She's hiring a health aid to help her with Melvin for a couple weeks.

"I used to do that in Minnesota."

"Why haven't you taken it up here?"

"My husband became ill and he takes up a lot of my time."

"Oh, I see." Ben paid for his tablets with cash, and Ruth locked up for the night, tired from boredom and relieved that she had a few days off.

• • •

That Saturday, Ruth caught up with a few chores and did some grocery shopping. She called the clinic in Minnesota on Monday to confirm Har's yearly physical checkup. Their health insurance, which was part of their pension plan, was paid mostly by the mining company, but an annoying stipulation required them to be residents of Minnesota for part of the year. Ruth worked around that requirement by using the Minnesota address of her most trusted friend for correspondence with the insurance company. Har never complained, but he submitted to the physical passively. Ruth always scheduled her own checkups for the same time. As far as the insurance company knew, they were snowbirds who spent winters in Oregon and summers in Hibbing.

After lunch, she finished writing a letter and made out a few checks to pay bills, then meandered around the ten acres that surrounded her house. She walked slowly, worrying about forest fires. There had already been a few, but luckily they'd been extinguished before growing large. The tall pines around Ruth's house seemed almost as if they were red flags waving in the wind to attract a lightning strike, even though they rarely had thunderstorms near the coast. She shook her head, brushing aside her imaginary worries. She had plenty of actual ones to occupy her mind.

Close to the house she stopped to admire her favorite carving. A tree, dead and free of bark, had broken off about ten feet above the ground. Har had filled the tree with carvings, totem-pole style, of the Virgin Mary in various moods. Not a single one featured her as the serene young woman she was usually depicted as being. In one, Mary appeared to be exhausted and another showed her with a Mona Lisa smile, with eyes squinting wickedly. But in Ruth's favorite, she looked seriously pissed off. No matter how cruddy Ruth felt, that one always made her grin.

Chapter 8

DURING THE EVENINGS OF late September, the many-windowed rooms in Rachel's house became spooky black holes, creeping her out. Only the formal living room had draperies, but they didn't use that room because it still had no furniture in it.

In the master bedroom, Rachel slid flat sheets onto the rods of the four large windows, creating a temporary, multi-colored solution, which left them only one top sheet for the bed. She became uneasy when she had to walk through the other rooms after dark, imagining a cougar licking his chops as he watched her move around inside the house. There was no way she could wait for the heavy rains before she made the curtains, as had been her original plan.

There were no fabric stores in Crusty Beach, and she didn't feel like driving all the way to Medford, so she found a factory outlet online and ordered fabric and pleating tape for the bedroom, master bath, and dining room drapes. For her breakfast nook, she bought sheer panels that only had to be shortened. After she hung them, the room looked homey, as if someone actually lived there. During the daylight hours she pushed them aside so she could see the little patch of ocean, becoming impatient for the rains so she could shoot off a few more branches and enlarge the view. She hoped to eventually drop one or two trees, increasing her view still more.

She set up her Singer on the dining room table for the project, worried that she might have forgotten how to sew. In five long days she finished all the draperies; her skills had readily come back.

It rained constantly for three days at the end of the month. Rachel was at loose ends, and she needed a break after sewing, so she made a batch of cardamom biscuits, working off her dissatisfaction by kneading. Then she called Ruth.

"Nick's painting his greenhouse tables, and I wondered if you'd like company for an hour or so."

"Sure, why not? Follow the stone path to my back door. Be careful on the bridge. It's as slick as greased Teflon when it's wet, and those rickety rails won't hold back a mouse."

Rachel left a note on the table for Nick and wrapped a ring of warm biscuits in paper towels, her dish towels being disgustingly grungy. She slipped into an old cardigan, grabbed her umbrella, and left. The stream had risen a little, gurgling as it splashed its way to the sea. The bridge *was* slippery, so she inched her way across it.

Ruth opened the door before she knocked, and Rachel entered a large back hall, from which carpeted stairs rose. She glimpsed a living room to the right as she took off her shoes and sweater. Ruth left her umbrella open, hanging it on the newel post to dry.

"Mmm, this sure smells good," Ruth said, sniffing the wrapped bundle Rachel handed to her. "And I just made a fresh pot of coffee to go with it." She led the way through a hall, past three closed doors, and into the aqua kitchen.

"This reminds me of my grandma's farmhouse. The kitchen is practically identical except for the colors."

"I inherited the place from one of my aunts, or we probably wouldn't have retired here or even thought of it. Har had a hankering for the desert."

Rachel said, "Not my thing."

"Nor mine."

Rachel sat down at the square table, while Ruth poured coffee. They sat down, sampling the biscuits and Ruth's spicy molasses cookies made from wholewheat flour. After Rachel wrote down the recipe, she asked, "How long have you lived here?"

"This will be my, uh, our third winter. What made *you* decide on Oregon?"

"We were looking in Texas, but a tornado slammed down near us while we were there. California is too expensive and Florida too moldy. We took a trip here and fell in love with the area." She took a sip of coffee. "Nick worked in the mines in management, so he has a good pension."

Ruth nodded. "Har also worked in management—near Hibbing—so it's the same with us. I didn't work long enough to get a pension, and it'll be twelve or fifteen years before I'm eligible for Social Security, so he'd better stay alive until then."

"Don't you get a hefty portion of his pension if he should die?"

"Yeah, some, but certainly not hefty; it'll only be a little over a hundred a month."

Rachel's mouth fell open in surprise. "I thought it was more. The women I know get about half of what their husbands brought in after they retired *and* continuing health insurance at low cost." She bumped her sore elbow on the edge of the table and rubbed it unobtrusively to ease the pain.

Looking disgusted, Ruth said, "I used to think so too. One mining company actually reneged all promises when it declared bankruptcy. Worst of all, if you retire early you lose that option. Better check through those stacks of paper you got when he left work."

"Oh, great."

"Amen to that. More coffee?"

Rachel accepted and said, "Hibbing. Home of Bob Dylan. Did you ever meet him?"

"It's possible, but he'd have been just an older kid. Quite a bit older. Anyway, he left for the Twin Cities way before I was old enough to think romantically about boys."

"What can you tell me about earthquakes here?"

"There's been only a mild one since we got here," Ruth said. "It gave the house a little creaking jerk and my glassware tinkled a bit, just like during a mine blast. That's what I thought it was until the next day when my boss asked if I'd felt the quake."

They spent a couple of pleasant hours learning more about each other, before Rachel left at dusk.

• • •

Nick brought home an older guy he met while he was beachcombing. Archie collected agates, which he tumbled and polished, then sold to the tourists in the summer. He often came over to help Nick unload driftwood. They usually came in for coffee, and Rachel would have liked to meet his wife, but she hadn't yet retired and had little time to socialize. Still, she was relieved that Nick had a companion for his walks, because she worried when he left to walk on distant beaches. He took his medications and seemed fine, but now and then he shuffled his feet when he walked, though only for a step or two. Other than that, he'd had no symptoms.

What Ruth had mentioned about Har's pension troubled her, so she dug out the box of Nick's retirement papers and began to choke her way through them. They were almost as incomprehensible as the instructions for the Federal tax returns, but she eventually came to understand that what Ruth told her was true. Her bowels twisted with anxiety. If Nick died now, she'd get less than a hundred dollars a month from his pension. And, until she could find a job, it would be her total income. She vowed to do her best to keep her husband healthy.

Chapter 9

RUTH DROVE HER SMALL RV to Minnesota for Har's checkup. Late September and October, with their moderate temperatures and roads mostly free of tourists, were her favorite months to travel. She made the trip from Crusty Beach to Hibbing in two *long* days, planning to tour Montana at a more leisurely pace on the way back, wishing to see a bit of Glacier Park before it melted. It would have been easier if Har drove, but he stubbornly refused to even get on the riding mower, though he willingly used the push mower for the entire acre of lawn.

His checkup indicated that he was stable and could continue to take the same blood-pressure medication. Her physical was also unremarkable. Finished with the yearly chore, she drove to her friend's house in Hibbing. She parked alongside the garage in the shady yard, made Har a ham and cheese sandwich, and then strolled around Angela's oversized yard, waiting for her to get home from her job.

"You look just the same!" Angie said, giving her a hug.

Ruth smiled wryly. "Well, hell, I thought I'd improved. You have. That's a good haircut you've got."

"Thanks. There's a new girl working at Curls." They walked around the back yard admiring the fine crop of apples her Haarleson trees had produced. "How are yours doing?"

"I have more than I can use, but there's a special refrigerator in the garage that keeps them fresh until about February. I have a full basket for you in the RV."

They drifted toward the back door. Angela asked, "Will Har be all right by himself?"

"Yeah. He's watching a movie and eating a sandwich. He prefers being alone."

"Any changes in his condition?"

"He's no worse and he's no better. I managed to get power of attorney, though, and that's made things a hell of a lot easier. I'm grateful that you're willing to let us use your address for our insurance and pension correspondence."

"You'd do it for me."

They had coffee and a salad supper, catching up on what their mutual acquaintances were doing. Ruth gave Angie a rug that she'd hooked, replete with purple irises, which her friend accepted with joy. They stayed up late talking, and thrill of thrills, after days of washing up in the tiny RV bathroom, Ruth used Angela's whirlpool tub and relaxed her tense and achy body.

Early the next morning, they were on the road, heading west. They explored Montana for five days. Although it was nearby, she left Yellowstone for another time.

• • •

They'd been home for only three days when it began to rain; the forecast promised drizzle for a week. After two days of being stuck in her house, she called Rachel and arranged to visit her that afternoon.

Ruth hung her gray trench coat up on the coat rack and looked around curiously. "I never visited the last people who lived here. They were nice enough, but only in their late twenties, and I was antique and apparently invisible to them."

"One of the thrills of aging," said Rachel. She gave her a tour of the house. "We can't afford any more furniture until we get the mortgage paid off, but that won't be forever. Actually, it's enough, unless our daughters decide to visit."

"Do you like all these white walls?" She pushed her freshly colored hair behind her ears.

"No. It reminds me of snow. Ick!"

Ruth laughed. "Amen to that. The last spring we were in Minnesota, it snowed on Mother's Day and then winter started early with a dusting on Labor Day."

"I remember that one." She shivered. "I'm not sure how I'm going to handle all the rain. I wish we could have moved to southern California, except for the pollution and the earthquakes. Mostly, it was too expensive." She led them into the breakfast nook, where there were two chairs with yellow cushions at the table holding her computer.

"Sit. I'll get us some coffee."

Ruth glanced around the room and gazed out the windows from which the curtains were drawn open.

"Oh, you can see the ocean! I can too, but only from my upstairs storage room."

Rachel placed sunflower-yellow mugs filled with coffee on the table and went to stand by Ruth. "Do you know who owns the land below ours?"

"Ah, not personally, but it's supposed to be owned by a wealthy couple from California. They have ten or twenty acres but haven't so much as put up a doghouse yet."

With sparkling eyes, Rachel said, "I'll confess then; I didn't have the ocean view until I started shooting branches off the trees down there."

Ruth laughed uproariously. "I wondered who was shooting. I wouldn't mind seeing more of the Pacific myself," she said, grinning widely. "Maybe we could thin the forest out a little here and there so I could."

They sat down. "The next day that it doesn't rain, let's go see what size trees we have to deal with. I don't think I'll tell my husband. He can be such a stickler about the legality of things."

Ruth chatted about her trip to Minnesota for Har's checkup and explained how Angela was forwarding her paperwork.

"Your secret is safe with me; my oldest daughter is doing that for us. Birds of a feather, we are indeed. Say, do you happen to know anything about our neighbor across the road?"

"Vivian? We don't visit, but we chitchat when we meet at the mailbox. She's looking to snag a man with money."

"I can't damn her for that. After what I found out about Nick's pension, Vivian may eventually have some serious competition. I won't even get a hundred bucks a month."

"What you have to do," Ruth said, "is make certain that your husband doesn't die until you can afford it. No matter what, don't let him die." She didn't dare say more.

Rachel stared at her. "I *am* doing my part with diet and encouraging him to exercise, but what the hell, when your time is up, its up."

Nick stomped into the house from the breezeway, and Rachel introduced him to Ruth. "Nick is putting one of those electric saunas in the corner of the garage, along with a shower and toilet. It's our Christmas gift to each other. We'll never use all three stalls for vehicles."

"Oh, that sounds *nice*." She grinned at them. "I'm a full-blooded Finn who hasn't had a sauna for three years. Hint, hint."

"You'll be our first guest," said Nick with a chuckle. "It probably won't be done until spring, so don't hold your breath." He went into the family room and turned on the television.

Ruth glanced at her watch. "Time to go. Please, drop by anytime. It'll help us keep our sanity during the rainy season. And, it's healthier than drinking straight whiskey."

At home, Ruth prepared some scalloped potatoes with ham, one of Har's favorite suppers. She hoped that Nick had a long life because she liked Rachel and didn't want to lose her as a neighbor and a friend. But if the worst should happen to Nick, she could help Rachel cope, plus help her hang onto her house and the entire pension. Rachel seemed like enough of a rebel to perform the somewhat unorthodox actions needed to keep what she had.

Chapter 10

IN EARLY OCTOBER RACHEL examined the guesthouse, hoping it was sturdy enough for a summer rental. The cottage was located across the creek and down the slope, close to the split-rail fence that marked the property line. The modest, square building had a porch running the full length of the west side, from which a pair of French doors opened. The roof was new and the building, though needing paint, seemed solid.

She entered the musty-smelling kitchen, felt around the wall and flipped on the light switch, but to no avail. The previous owner had shut the breakers off, she recalled. Peering around the gloomy room, she located the electrical box by the refrigerator. She pushed the lever up and was rewarded by the overhead light above the sink glowing harshly. Taped to the kitchen wall was a list outlining the steps to take when opening and closing the cabin. Not needing anything but the lights, she skimmed the list and snapped them all on.

The cottage was basically two rooms: a combination kitchen and living area with a small bathroom and a bank of closets dividing it from the bedroom. All the walls were painted flat antique gold. There were no curtains, just yellowed shades. The floor planks were avocado green. The trim and the battered wooden kitchen cabinets had been painted burnt orange, giving the cottage a '70's look. A picture of her childhood home flickered through her mind, leaving her with a flash of nostalgia.

The chrome kitchen chairs needed new seat covers to replace the cracked red vinyl, but the Formica table was in good condition. A dust-colored couch in the living area looked so suspiciously verminous, she didn't dare sit down on it. Black-painted cable rolls served as end tables. Another cable roll was placed by the double bed, a deep-brown metal creation that had an exposed coil spring tentatively supporting a hideously stained, prison-like mattress that sagged into a deep valley. Rachel pushed down on the mattress and was rewarded with a cacophony of squeaks as the ancient spring lurched drunkenly forward and backward, then side to side. She wiped her hand on her pants, wrinkled her nose and backed away from the lively bed, bumping into a portable, electric space heater.

Having seen her fill, she turned off the breakers and stepped into the porch. Visible through some leafless branches was the wonderful Pacific Ocean, with a somewhat better view than she had in her breakfast nook. More branches to prune, she decided with a grin. Or maybe a controlled burn next summer. But that was too risky with the wind generally blowing from the west, right onto her property.

She wandered back to the bridge and went home, mulling over the best way to use the cottage. Nick had mentioned that it would be great to have it for Barbara and Denise when they visited with their boyfriends. As much as Rachel loved her daughters, she was realistic about how opportunistic they both were. She had a pretty good hunch that they might become permanent houseguests if a free cabin were available.

A better idea would be to rent it out to some writer or artist during the summer months when heating it wouldn't be a problem. Of course she'd have to spiff it up and get some newer furniture in there.

• • •

She mentioned this when she and Nick took ten days off at the end of October and drove down the coastal highways of California, sleeping in their camper.

"A summer rental would bring income, and we could put a Franklin stove in the living room in case we got renters in the winter. We have two unused bedrooms in the house, so it isn't like we need it for *our* company."

"What's the absolute minimum that it would take to fix it up?" Nick asked. His brown hair had begun to thin a little, but he hadn't grayed much.

She thought for a minute. "Paint the walls and ceilings. Replace the bed and the couch. Staple new vinyl onto the kitchen chairs. The bathroom is fine, but it needs a good scrubbing. Curtains, or at least valances would be nice. The Franklin stove could come later, and we wouldn't have to put up a chimney, just one of those insulated stovepipes."

Nick said, "If we bought most of it used it wouldn't cost all that much either."

"We could do the work during this winter and rent it out in the spring."

"I suppose you want me to paint."

"Yes, but only the walls and ceiling. I'll have you do it all in off-white and I'll tape around the trim for you."

He looked disgruntled.

"I'd do it, except it would retard the healing on my elbow."

"Oh, all right, all right."

She didn't mention that it would most likely take two or possibly even three coats.

The California landscape, with its spectacular views of the Pacific, was endlessly fascinating for Rachel, who'd never seen the ocean before moving to Oregon. When they were halfway through the state, they left the clouds behind. Ignoring most of the usual tourist attractions, Nick and Rachel stopped instead at many of the beaches, the ocean offering what interested them most. When they reached San Diego, they spent a night at a motel, needing the air conditioning.

Rachel stretched out in the king-size bed and reached onto the bedside dresser for her cherry-scented lip balm and smeared it onto her chapped lips. She handed it to Nick, who used it and gave it back.

"Boy is the humidity low here," he said, rubbing his lips together. "I miss the rain forest."

"Me too," she said. "I miss not having any maple trees this fall with their gorgeous reds and oranges. The leaves turned mostly shades of yellow around Crusty Beach."

"Yeah, but I sure don't miss the cold."

"Me either. The cold goes right through you."

Chapter 11

VIVIAN WAS DISGUSTED WITH the blubber that kept piling up on her frame. Her belly had always been a magnet for fat, but a panty girdle had conveniently taken care of it. This fall, however, the fat had spread over her entire torso and even more heavily on her stomach. Now, her panty girdle created an ugly roll of squished-up fat above her waist. She chewed a stalk of celery, pretending it was heaped with cream cheese and olives. If she were married, it wouldn't matter if she were a bit chubby. She'd stuff her husband with food until he was downright fat, so she could quit starving herself. But, until that lucky day, the fat had to go.

It was Sunday, one of her days off, and naturally it was drizzling. Dusty was outside with his friend Brian Pearson, working under a blue plastic tarp they had draped over some poles and duct-taped onto the roof of the aging mobile home. It made a dry work area for the car they were supposedly overhauling, but the tarp cast an unpleasant blue light into the living room, where she'd painted the imitation wood paneling a decided shade of turquoise. The glut of blue made her skin look positively gangrenous.

Vivian went to the kitchen and slid a pan of cornbread into the oven. The chili had already begun to bubble, so she lowered the temperature. The smell of the spicy meal made her ravenous, so she chomped her way through another stalk of celery. She opened the back door and was blasted by rock music. "Turn that down!"

Dusty shut the radio off without protest.

"Lunch in ten minutes. Do you like chili, Brian?"

"Oh, yeah. Lots." He had a repulsively thin, weasel-like face and his frail limbs resembled toothpicks held together with knobs of chewing gum. His brown freckles looked like they'd been splattered on from a mud puddle.

Dusty wiped his hands on a rag and said, "We should have this car done before March. Brian helped his older brothers with their cars, so he knows what to do."

"Good." Vivian figured it was better than growing pot or chasing girls, though she figured girls were right down the road. And soon, there would be the expense of car insurance for a teen. At least he was on the honor roll. She stepped back into the house and set the table.

They were passing the food around when she casually asked Brian, "How long have you lived in Crusty Beach?" She didn't especially care, but her stomach growled like an old cement mixer at the quiet table, and conversation masked it.

"Seven years," he said, buttering a slab of cornbread. "We moved here after mom died and stayed with our grandparents. Dad works road construction. He's home only four months of the year, plus most weekends."

Guys on road construction made damn good wages. She studied Brian and concluded that he looked homely because he was too thin, something easily remedied. "How many brothers and sisters do you have?" She had no desire to become a stepmother to a huge brood of kids, no matter how much money their father made.

"Two brothers. They both live in Idaho and are married."

Vivian took tiny nibbles of chili from her modest portion, chewing and chewing, then swallowing each mouthful with sips of water so it would seem like more. *Should I ask? Better not.* "Has your dad remarried?" She couldn't resist.

Brian wasn't nearly as unattractive as she'd first thought. He looked rather wholesome with his reddish-blonde hair and sprinkling of freckles across his nose and cheeks. She'd just bet that he took after his dad.

"No. And Grandpa died last year, so now it's usually just me and Grandma in that big house."

Perhaps Brian's dad would inherit that big house. It might be one of those rundown Victorian houses that filled the town. They were too good to condemn, but shabby, since the residents didn't have the money to maintain them. Still, anything was better than their trailer. And Granny *must* be getting close to the age where she was ready for a nursing home.

The boys cleaned out the kettle and ate all the cornbread except a sliver the size of two fingers. They dug out a carton of peppermint ice cream. Vivian refused to even taste the treat she loved so dearly, but she encouraged the boys to take large portions. Brian's dad might be grateful if she could put a little roundness on his son's hatchet-thin face. She piled the dishes into the sink to soak, then sat down with a cup of coffee while they spooned down their ice cream.

"Where exactly do you live?"

"On Eagle Point Road, close to the ocean. It's that big stone house with the round tower."

Vivian felt her heart begin to pound more rapidly. "I know where it's at." She kept her voice smooth and socially polite. "It's a very nice house." Nice was an understatement; the place sat on about three acres and was landscaped to perfection. And there had to be at least five bedrooms in the place, more than enough room for her and Dusty.

She labored to keep the avaricious expression off her face. "What time do you have to be home?" she asked Brian.

"About three. Grandma said to call if it was raining and she'd pick me up."

"Well, being as I have to pick up a few groceries this afternoon, I'll drive you home."

"Hey, thanks."

After they went back outside, Vivian hurried through the dishes before going to the bathroom to wipe off most of her makeup. She was wearing old brown cords, which looked respectable, but she changed the orange turtleneck for a tan blouse. Finally, she twisted her hair into a tight bun.

Vivian planned to check out Granny Pearson, to determine if she'd be a friend or foe when Vivian attempted to snag her son, whose name was still unknown.

Chapter 12

DURING THE RAINS OF November, Rachel bought two secondhand wicker rockers for the cottage and made cushions for them. She sewed valances for the kitchen and living areas, and then made full curtains for the bedroom and bath, using flat queen-size sheets.

Nick painted the walls and ceiling during the early part of the month, when it was still quite warm. He grumbled so much about having to roll on a second coat, that Rachel helped him, first wrapping her elbow in an elastic bandage to prevent further strain to the joint.

"Why did you choose this dirty-looking white?" he asked.

"It's not dirty, it's cream. It'll look better with the old kitchen appliances."

The ceiling had required only one coat, but the dark-gold walls were tough to cover. Rachel inspired herself to finish the job by visualizing the clean brightness of the rooms when she was done. She'd bought celery-green paint to do the trim and cabinets after the walls were finished, thinking it would harmonize with the deeper green paint on the floor. If the cabin looked good, she'd be able to charge enough for rent to have the exterior painted and still have some money left over. Also, if she were able to rent it out for all but the four coldest months, they'd be able to put some money aside to travel in Nevada and Arizona next winter. Dreaming about that gave her the energy to finish the kitchen before she stopped for a cup of tea.

Nick joined her, rubbing his right shoulder. "I've done so little physical work since we moved here that I'm getting out of shape. I better start doing a few exercises tomorrow morning."

"Me too. This house is a lot easier to care for than our old one, and I've put on a few pounds."

Rachel poured water from a saucepan into a pair of mismatched cups and placed them on the table. She dug a handful of assorted tea bags from her jacket pocket and brewed green tea for herself. Nick chose mint.

"We could ask some of our friends to stay here in the summer. They could have long vacations rent free and really explore the area," he said.

"I thought it was to rent out for money."

"We can do that too, for the months our friends aren't here."

Rachel kept silent. She did the paperwork and knew how close they were living to the edge of their income. If company did stay, Nick would expect her to provide the lavish meals she'd always served in the days when they'd both worked and had the money to do so.

They couldn't do that and still have any vacation money for next winter. And, with gasoline prices rising so steadily, consumer goods would go up accordingly. But to ensure his help with the rest of the painting, she didn't point out that renting the guesthouse was not merely for mad money. A better time would be after they had paid their real-estate taxes, when Nick was feeling broke and resentful. She finished her tea and went back to work.

• • •

The following day she asked Ruth where the property line jumped the creek and if she minded her and Nick, and possible guests, using the trail that was on her land.

"I gather that my aunt needed money after her husband died and sold the cottage to the then owners of your house. There's a permanent easement along the creek that goes along with it," Ruth answered.

"Nick worries about the septic system being so close to the creek."

Ruth chuckled. "That was grandfathered in. Don't worry about it."

"Where does the drinking water come from? We couldn't find a well."

"It shoots off of our line. It'll never amount to much, since the place will never house more than two people at a time. It's written down in all that legal paperwork that's with the sale of the house."

Rachel was grateful that she liked Ruth so much, and any problems would easily be solved between them, without dragging an expensive lawyer into it. But if she should move. . .

• • •

A furniture store in Medford had a good sale on beds, so they purchased a pair of double-size mattresses and box springs. The company truck delivered them, but the frames were on back order. After stashing them in one of the spare bedrooms, she relaxed a bit. Both of the girls and their boyfriends had made tentative plans to visit during Thanksgiving, and now she had something for them to sleep on. Even if the frames hadn't arrived by then, she could put the mattresses on the floor, since young people had little trouble sleeping. She got a large turkey and made menu plans.

Two days before the holiday, a huge snowstorm hit the Midwest, and their flight was cancelled. Rachel felt both relieved and disappointed. As much as she would have liked to see them, she felt tired, as if she were coming down with the flu. The days passed and she didn't get sick, but she finally realized that her exhaustion came from not sleeping well. Nick had some difficulty staying asleep since his strokes, and he read when he couldn't doze off again. Rachel could not sleep with the light on. She bought a sleep mask, but it put slight pressure against her eyeballs, which created such peculiar swirls of brilliantly colored lights that *they* kept her awake.

One night in desperation she dragged an extra quilt out of the blanket chest and hauled it into one of the extra bedrooms. She hadn't yet made curtains for the room, but she was so exhausted that she didn't care if a cougar looked in. She slid the closest mattress onto the floor, tore the plastic cover off and lay down, tucking the quilt snuggly around her feet. She was too tired to even get a pillow.

And she slept, deeply, for nearly twelve hours.

When she finally rose, she felt ten years younger.

At the breakfast table, Nick said, "You know they say the marriage is over when a couple no longer share the same bed."

He looked a little disgruntled.

"*They* can try to sleep with someone who reads for half the night. And then *they* can stuff it."

"Hmmph."

Chapter 13

ON A FOGGY MORNING in December, Ruth dressed in a ragged, gray sweat suit and armed herself with the old crosscut saw from her woodshed. She met Rachel, who was wearing patched jeans topped by a stretched-out black sweater and carrying an ax. They tromped down the hill on Ruth's side of the creek, searching for the hemlock with the top veering to the left that blocked Ruth's view of the ocean.

"You're positive the owners won't show up here at this time of year?" Rachel asked, peering nervously around the woods.

"The only time I've ever seen them around is in the summer. Heard them, actually. Two guys. They were camping on the property, talking about building in three years. The breeze blew their voices right into my back yard."

"Sounds like it'll be safe. Nobody in their right mind would hike through these soggy woods in the winter."

"We're here."

"That's proof we can use insanity as a defense."

They rambled through the forest and came across the hemlock that *appeared* to be the right one. From where they stood, however, nearly all of the hemlocks looked like potential candidates. Ruth took a bottle of olive oil and a rag from her pocket and coated the saw blade liberally.

Rachel gazed at her quizzically.

"I don't know why I'm doing it, but my grandfather did the same thing, except he smeared it with used car oil and kerosene."

After examining the tree carefully, Ruth had them kneel down on the west side, and they began to saw. The blade kept jumping out of the shallow notch until Rachel hacked a deeper trench with the ax. Then the saw stayed in place, but their progress was slow. After nearly an hour, they hadn't even sawed six inches into the fifteen-inch tree trunk. Suddenly, the tree leaned onto the blade and it got stuck. They pulled, kicked, and cussed, and Ruth even prayed in desperation, but the saw wouldn't budge.

"Damn!" Rachel said, and collapsed onto the pine needle covered ground. "Any chance the owner would believe that it just grew that way?"

"The dumbest ass from the desert would never believe this happened naturally," Ruth said, slumping down onto the slightly damp ground. "Any other suggestions?"

"I guess we'll have to chop the tree down a little above the blade and get the saw out after it falls."

"Sounds like a plan," Ruth said. "You chop first."

"How sweet of you."

They took turns chopping and were barely halfway through the tree when it began to groan. They sped away and crouched behind an enormous Douglas fir while the tree tilted slowly downhill. It slammed down with a mighty crash that shook the ground.

"Sons-a-bitch!" Ruth said. "I hope no one heard that."

They stood silently, waiting for someone to burst from the woods to investigate what had happened, but no one came. They were able to pry the saw from the stump with ease, and began to saw the tree into lengths they could roll and drag up to Ruth's woodshed.

After the first five-foot log was cut, Rachel slowly eyeballed the tree, clipped her sweaty hair away from her face, and said, "It looks a hell of a lot longer when it's on the ground. I can't imagine how many hours it'll take us to cut up the whole thing."

Wearily, they rolled the log up the hill, maneuvering it around trees and brush. Finally, they reached the yard and parked it in front of the woodshed.

Rachel peeled off her black sweater and threw it on the ground. She held her navy T-shirt away from her chest in an effort to cool off.

Ruth stripped off her sweatshirt, revealing a stained mauve turtleneck. She bent forward from her waist, panting from exertion. Tiredly, they started back down the hill to retrieve their logging gear. "We need some help," she said, examining the blisters on her hands. "How about your husband?"

Rachel walked beside her. "He's one of those guys who won't even break the speeding laws. And he knows where the property lines run. How about yours? Is he well enough?"

"Yeah, but only for splitting and stacking it."

"Damn." She scooped up some moss and draped it on the freshly cut stump, artificially speeding up the look of age. "Well, we sure as hell can't leave it here. How about if we hire that Snell kid? Vivian said he does odd jobs. And it'd be unlikely for him to know about the property lines."

Ruth said, "Good idea. First let's go see how my ocean view looks."

Unfortunately, it didn't look any better, because they'd cut down the wrong tree.

"Vivian always gets her mail at 11:30, and it's almost that now. Let's go talk to her."

She was at the mailbox when they got there, her hair hanging down her back in loose red curls suitable for a much younger woman from a much earlier era.

"Do you think Dusty would do some outside chores for us on the nicer days this winter?" Ruth asked.

"He could, but he's overhauling a car. He gets his license this spring, and cars are his life. I couldn't hardly get him to haul out the garbage this morning." She paused, wrinkling her forehead. "If you can wait till he needs to buy gas ..."

They all laughed.

Rachel said, "Maybe we'll just put an ad in the paper instead."

Vivian left, clutching a handful of envelopes.

Ruth grabbed her mail. "Well, hell, now what? I'm too tired to think of anything else. I suppose we'll have to put that ad in."

"I just said that to keep Vivian off the track. If we run an ad, we might get someone who knows the owners."

"I never thought of that. It's supposed to be nice all week—warm and no rain. Why don't we just go out every day and chop down a few more trees."

Rachel grinned at her. "Why not? We know we're able to do *that*."

Ruth pondered it for a few seconds and nodded. "We can figure out the rest of it later."

Chapter 14

TWILIGHT CAME EARLY DURING the drizzly month of December, but Nick and Rachel quickly got into the habit of watching DVDs from their generous collection, many of which were still in wrappers. They usually had a light supper while they did so, and the screened porch kept the hungry cougars away from the double set of glass doors.

Rachel's fear of mountain lions had begun two winters before they left Minnesota when she'd come across a set of plate size tracks loping across the yard into the woods behind their house. The tracks had come within five *feet* of the deck, causing her to have slash and bite nightmares for weeks.

Nick opened a new DVD that he'd ordered, a recent drama both of them would enjoy. Rachel fetched the ham and cheese sandwiches she'd made for their casual supper, pouring each of them a cup of herbal tea. The contentment she'd felt at the beginning of the rainy season was turning to boredom at watching an endless series of movies.

While they waited for the previews to end, Nick took a sandwich and said, "You've been spending a lot of time with Ruth. Glad you two get along so well."

"Me too. I've been helping her do some pruning, cutting down some brush—small trees, actually. Will you show me how to use that electric chainsaw?" She spoke casually, giving him only enough information so it would sound like she was being truthful.

"Yeah, tomorrow, if it's not raining. Is there anything big? I could do it."

"No, not really. Old azaleas or something like that, Ruth said." Ruth *had* said something like that about her shrubs, but she certainly wouldn't want to cut them down. But if Nick knew what they were really doing, he'd insist that they quit, which she had no intention of doing.

She bit into her sandwich and watched the movie. Nick dropped the subject, and she felt relieved, often having difficulty keeping things from him.

• • •

The drizzle let up after two days, and Nick showed her how to operate the saw, including safety tips covering every conceivable eventuality. The entire lesson took approximately four minutes.

He said, "There's about four-hundred feet of heavy-duty extension cord in the garage, but if Ruth needs more, she can probably rent it from that equipment rental place in Crusty. The saw might lose power if she has a lot of cord, though."

"I'll remember that."

"I wish you'd let me do it."

"It seems silly when the shrubs aren't much taller than me."

Nick seemed unconvinced, but said, "Well, you know where I am if you need help."

• • •

That afternoon Rachel and Ruth paced off the distance from their houses down the hill to the farthest trees.

"Let's drive into town and see what that cord will cost to rent," said Ruth. "If it's really high, we'll get it for one day and work fast."

"Maybe they rent out garden tractors too. Rolling those logs up the hill is exhausting."

It started to rain again, though not hard. They took Ruth's car and it took only a few minutes to get to Crusty Rent-All, which was located on the outskirts of the small town. They hurried to the front door of the huge warehouse and went to a small, walled-off area that contained a desk, the till, and a youngish man with *William Julius, Proprietor* embroidered on his pocket in glowing fuchsia.

"Howdy, ladies. What can I do for you?"

"We're checking prices on heavy-duty extension cords," Ruth said. "We need to rent about twelve-hundred feet."

William didn't even blink. "You'll need a contractor's spool then. It's half price until the middle of March, when the professional builders start calling for it." He quoted a moderate price and suggested they haul it in a pickup truck, since the spool was too large to fit in the trunk.

"Do you have a lawn tractor or an ATV with a trailer to haul some firewood up a slope?" Rachel asked.

William took his hat off, looked them up and down and scratched his head. "Either of you ever driven an ATV?"

"We tore around on a pair of Bearcat 454's in Minnesota. We used to climb up the old mine dumps," Rachel said.

With a big grin, William slapped his hat back on. "Oh. Minnesota women. Okay. We'll have to install a set of chains for this time of year. Ground gets pretty soft from all the rain. Call a day ahead so we can put them on." The price for the wheeler was high, but not exorbitant. And he kindly told them the location of a trail so they could drive it home.

In the car, Ruth said, "Geez, if you'd piled it on any thicker, he'd have offered us jobs as high riggers at his brother's logging company."

Rachel chuckled. "What did that comment about Minnesota women mean?"

"No idea."

It was now pouring, so Ruth drove right up to Rachel's breezeway. Even though she raced in, her hat and hair got soaked and her jacket soggy. She kicked off her sopping shoes, the third pair she'd set aside to dry that day. She wondered how she was going to stand three more months of this. Virtually the only outdoor exercise she got was the logging that she and Ruth did on the drier days, and she was beginning to feel antsy.

Nick had the fire burning in the family room, which produced a warmer-feeling heat than the electric baseboards that served the house. He looked cozy in a pale blue terrycloth robe and jogging pants. Rachel greeted him, then went into the kitchen and took a kettle of homemade soup from the refrigerator. She stuck it on the burner to heat, adding some fresh parsley and a little water.

While she waited for it to warm, she folded a dryer load of towels and filled the washer with dark colors. The new bottle of laundry detergent wasn't in the cabinet where she'd put it, so she dug through all the cabinets in the room, but it had vanished. She gave the soup a stir and went back to the family room.

"Did you use the laundry detergent for something and not put it back?"

He looked up from a pile of DVDs from which he was removing the security tape, and said, "No. I haven't washed a single load of clothes since we moved here."

Rachel scratched her head. "It must be somewhere. I just bought it yesterday."

She looked through the pantry, the roomy closet in the powder room, where she stored extra supplies, and under the kitchen sink. Giving up her search, she grabbed the dishwashing liquid and squeezed a generous amount into the washer. She'd mislaid several things lately; it must be residual stress from the move that was causing her forgetfulness. She refused to consider the possibility of early dementia.

The sounds of a movie came on, and she wondered which one of their collection Nick had chosen for the night. It didn'treally matter, since it was mostly background noise to her efforts at teaching herself to appliqué, a pleasant, ladylike interest she pursued in the evenings to contrast with her day-time felonies.

Chapter 15

JEALOUSY FLARED THROUGH VIVIAN when she talked with Ruth and Rachel about hiring Dusty for some odd jobs, although she hid it. She wished she were rich enough to hire someone to do a little of her yard work, maybe even plant some trees or put in a flower bed. All that her plot held was matted down crabgrass. And her sidewalk was an old black conveyor belt, which was dangerously slippery when wet. She tottered beside it now, not wanting to take a spill and then having to dig for something clean enough to wear to work. Something that fit.

In the house, she grimly chewed on celery while she braided her hair and pinned it up in a bun. Heaven help her if she dropped a single hair into someone's meal. She didn't bother with perfume; within an hour she'd reek of garlic-coated fried chicken, which was today's special. She placed a note on the table for Dusty and left, swerving around a water-filled pothole with her rusty old beater.

She arrived at work early, so she sat in the car and watched the rain make trails down the windshield, mulling over the day she'd driven Brian Pearson home. She'd expected Granny Pearson to be a white-haired old lady, with a mind only half there, but the energetic and fit woman who'd opened the door had sized her up instantly. She'd thanked her quite pleasantly but had not invited her in. Since then, Vivian hadn't come up with any other ideas to meet Brian's dad, so she crossed him off her list. Now she had little chance of meeting any men until the rainy season was over.

She trudged around puddles to the back door of the café and went inside. After she hung her coat up, she slipped on a black hairnet, deliberately avoiding looking in the mirror. She knew she looked like Olive Oyl, although one of the older waiters had once told her that she looked like a Madonna, which seemed even worse. Wearily she went into the kitchen and tied her apron on, wishing and hoping that she'd win a sweepstakes or a lottery or find a trunk full of money. While she fried endless baskets of chicken and fries, she dreamed about all the pleasant things she'd do if she were rich. Or even just a little wealthier.

Perhaps she could blackmail someone. The trouble was, she knew few people with secrets, and those few had secrets so trivial that they weren't worth anything. None of those people had any money to pay her anyway. She sighed and plunged another basket of coated chicken into the hot oil.

All evening she munched while she cooked, sticking with raw vegetables, eating only one deep-fried chicken thigh from which she discarded the crispy, fat-laden skin. At the café, they were allowed one free meal per shift, but they could nibble as much as they chose. Vivian wanted to gorge herself on the rich food, but that's what had made her gain so much in the first place. Lately, she'd been taking her gratis meal home and giving it to Dusty, to economize.

Jill worked near her, making salads, vegetable platters, and baskets of rolls. The café was so busy, they didn't have a moment to talk until closing time, when they collapsed into chairs at the salad-preparation table and shared a beer.

"This should be the last hectic night until New Years," Jill said. She gulped down some beer from her glass.

"Yeah," Vivian answered. "I need a break, but I need the money more. Anyways, will you tell that friend of yours that I'll watch her two-year-old? She can sleep on the couch." Now she'd *have* to clean the filthy thing, a job that had been long postponed.

"All right. It's really no big deal—he dumps her off on her way to the hospital at eleven and picks her up a little before eight in the morning. You just have to feed her breakfast."

"And like you said, she's potty trained, and it's only for two weeks."

• • •

The girl *was* easy to care for. She gazed at Dusty with adoring blue eyes, and he took a shine to her, entertaining her in the morning before he went to school, leaving only a few minutes she had to care for the girl before her mother picked her up. Vivian wished the regular babysitter would quit permanently, since this was a physically undemanding job she could easily finagle in with her schedule.

Unfortunately, the sitter came back as planned. Now, though, she had some money to buy Christmas gifts for Dusty and to pay some bills. The cash quickly melted away.

Feeling in need of some adult male companionship, Vivian answered three ads in the lonely-hearts column, even sending photos. Her heart sped up when she walked to her mailbox, but day after day passed with no replies. She became frustrated and ill tempered, wracking her brain to figure out just *what* in the hell she lacked.

Chapter 16

BEFORE THEY'D MOVED TO Oregon, Rachel had spent hours doing research about the region, including the climate. She felt certain she was prepared for the rains, in fact welcomed them after existing through decades of snow. But it so seldom stopped misting, drizzling, or pouring, that she felt as housebound as she had during the frigid Minnesota winters. Their house had wide eaves, which prevented the windows from being constantly spattered, for which she was grateful. The downside was that they cut down on the natural light, making the overcast days seem even gloomier than they actually were.

Nick felt equally trapped. He bought a used treadmill and set it up in the screened porch. It gave them both a way to burn off some calories in the fresh air without wearing a raincoat or carrying an umbrella.

On a rare dry day, a couple of weeks before Christmas, Rachel and Ruth sneaked into the woods to do a little logging. They chopped down a tree with the ax, planning to use the chainsaw only for cutting the felled trees into manageable lengths. They whacked off branches and threw them into the swollen creek, where they were instantly whisked downstream by the racing current.

"I imagine they'll end up in to the ocean," Rachel said as she watched them slip out of sight.

Ruth paused in her chopping and sat on the log to rest. Her crisp, platinum hair was pulled back into a short ponytail and her straight bangs had been recently trimmed.

Rachel unzipped her hooded sweatshirt and pulled it off her shoulders. She sat down near Ruth.

"Probably. They might pile up under one of those bridges further downstream, but the street maintenance crews from Crusty can loosen jams with a pole. At least they don't cause pollution. It's not like we're throwing in old Fords."

Rachel laughed. "I hope we can get rid of all this before the owners decide to pay a visit."

"We will. I sure like seeing the ocean from my living room windows."

"Nick finally noticed that he can see it, but he thinks it's because the leaves fell off the trees."

They worked for another hour, but then it clouded up and began to drizzle. They went to Rachel's for coffee, taking the blacktop to avoid the treacherously slick bridge.

They were standing in the kitchen waiting for the coffee to finish brewing when Nick came in from the greenhouse. He'd been mixing bags of peat moss, loam, and vermiculite to create a light potting soil.

"Hi, ladies," he said, digging his large, stainless steel cup out of the dishwasher. He filled it up, grabbed a handful of oatmeal cookies, and left, clutching his old black umbrella. The fabric flapped around a pair of missing spines, looking like a raven with a broken wing.

"He seems fine," Ruth said.

"Yes, he is, except for a slight limp now and then."

"Try to talk him into signing over power of attorney to you. It's easier to do before he loses his speech or worse, heaven forbid."

"I hate to even think about it."

"Just do it."

Rachel knew she'd be smart to heed Ruth's advice.

• • •

A week before Christmas, while they were eating lunch, Nick asked, "Aren't you putting up a tree?" He sprinkled Parmesan cheese onto his spaghetti.

"I hadn't planned on it. I gave all the decorations to the girls when we left."

He was plainly disappointed, although he'd never once helped with the holiday decorating or commented on what she'd done. When they'd moved, they had decided to discontinue the gift tradition and simply send cards. Rachel was happy to drop the outgrown holiday traditions they'd habitually practiced for years.

Nick, however, shuffled dispiritedly around the house for the remainder of the week, irritating Rachel with his sighs. But she refused to create piles of pointless work for herself by decorating a tree and putting up colored lights around the doors and windows.

She *did* buy a poinsettia from the grocery store and plunked it onto the middle of the dining room table. *There, that's festive enough,* she told herself.

Chapter 17

EVEN THOUGH SHE HAD only twenty bucks to live on for two weeks and was nearly out of groceries, Vivian refused to ask Dusty's father for an advance on her support check. That would be tantamount to giving him custody, since he'd accuse her of being financially incompetent and attempt to get custody of their son for the two remaining years before he turned eighteen. Her ex was absolutely the last person she'd turn to.

The ads she'd answered from the lonely-hearts column, on which she'd pinned a good deal of hope, hadn't netted any replies. Not a single knight, not even a chubby one wedged into tarnished armor, had responded. She could expect no aid from that quarter.

She scratched her head, sighed, and then wiped down a prep table in the kitchen at the restaurant, trying to keep busy during the post-holiday slump. Her mind was totally preoccupied with making money. The only other kitchen employee at the café was Helen, a woman nearly her age, widowed and working to pay her way for a move to Arizona.

Vivian asked, "Is there anything in the cooler that we'd better use up? I'm short of food and money."

"There's a lot of cheese, so we can take some of that without it being missed. But the only plentiful frozen meats are chicken nuggets and strips."

"Good enough. I'll only have to buy a few groceries."

They filled two bags with food, adding toilet paper from the supply closet.

"Good thing we don't have to do this very often," Helen said. "If that skinflint boss of ours would give out a holiday bonus, I wouldn't ever do this." She hauled both bags out to their cars while Vivian held Helen's umbrella over them. They scampered back into the kitchen to do a little more cleaning before quitting time. After finishing, they had coffee and croissants filled with deep-fried shrimp, which were horrendously high in calories, but Vivian was *hungry*.

"Why do you want to live in Arizona, besides the dry weather?" Vivian asked. She opened her croissant and fanned the shrimp with a paper napkin.

"I have a cousin who lives there. She's quite well off, and she'll let me live in the apartment above her three-stall garage, so I'll only have to pay utilities. She has a tennis court and a swimming pool."

"You'll roast in the summers."

"No, I won't. My cousin wants a companion to explore the northern part of the country with her during the warm months. She had a mastectomy, and her husband left her. She's not interested in another man, but she doesn't want to travel alone."

"Boy, you got it made! Why don't you go right away?"

"I need a newer car. And, I'm having trouble selling my house; they don't move fast here in the winter." She ate the last of her croissant and drank down her coffee, patting her mouth with a paper towel.

Vivian was a little envious of Helen. She owned a two-bedroom cottage, free and clear. Although rather small, it was on a triple lot only four blocks from the ocean. She'd easily be able to retire from the proceeds.

They closed the kitchen and locked up. The rain had quit, but the fog was rolling in, and Vivian had to inch home. She lugged the groceries in and put them away. Despite it being late, the boys were working on the car. Since tomorrow wasn't a school day, Brian was spending the night. Knowing they'd be ravenous, Vivian placed a package of chicken strips into the oven and added a frozen pumpkin pie to thaw.

While they heated, she sat at the table and mulled over the most recent plans she'd made for herself after Dusty graduated and left for technical college. Her dream was to move to Las Vegas, where she knew she could snag a wealthy man who'd come to gamble. She still looked pretty good, but the clock was ticking and wrinkles were sprouting on her face. With that thought, she stopped frowning and slapped a piece of scotch tape between her eyebrows as a reminder to keep her face placid. She wanted to leave now, but she couldn't, not until Dusty left. She loved him dearly, but there was no way she'd get a man to believe she was twenty-six if her big, bearded son lived with her. Besides, he'd be better off living with his father while attending college, something she had yet to discuss with the two of them.

Like Helen, she'd need a newer car when she moved. She wouldn't get much for her old trailer, but the lot was large, and it would give her a small stake. Too bad there were no eligible men around to give her some assistance. For her, life had always sucked.

She turned the chicken strips over with a spatula, mixed up a bowl of sweet and sour sauce for it, then called the boys in to eat. They talked briefly, and then Vivian left to watch a romance movie in her bedroom, taking a sliver of the pumpkin pie for a treat. She got tears in her eyes during the sad parts of the movie, but they were for her, not the heroine, for whom life also sucked, but only temporarily.

Chapter 18

RUTH HAD STARTED TO clean up after lunch when someone knocked on the front door. She opened it to Vivian, who pointed at a piece of driftwood she'd propped against the stair rail. "Someone drug this into the café, knowing I live close to the guy who does the Virginal carvings."

"Oh, thank you. Would you like some tea?" She stepped back from the door so Vivian could enter.

"Better not. My son broke his ankle at school yesterday, and he can't move around too good."

"He should heal fast. Kids usually do."

"Yeah, I guess." She backed up a step. "How's your husband doing? I used to see him walking up the road a lot, but not lately."

"He's the same, though I notice he's been rubbing his knee a lot recently. I suppose his arthritis is bothering him a little. He'll never communicate verbally, but luckily, his stroke affected nothing else. Thanks again for bringing the driftwood. He has only a few pieces left."

Vivian plucked her umbrella out of the rack and left, her orange raincoat a shrill note of color in the misty, muted landscape.

• • •

Har's supply of driftwood *was* running low, and the boys who'd usually collected it for him had moved away. Ruth asked Rachel and Nick if they'd go beachcombing with her when the current storm was over. "I'll check the tide tables and we'll go when it's low. I gather that most of those sneaker waves come in the winter," she said, adding, "and dress warmly. The wind off the ocean feels like it came from Minnesota."

They went, keeping their eyes open for sneaker waves, tsunamis, and earthquakes, which could conceivably tear the beach away from the mainland. They also stayed away from the banks, should they collapse. And, they carefully skirted the logs strewn on the beach. Between all the potential dangers, they did manage to find a few pieces of driftwood, the only casualty being one of Ruth's shoelaces breaking. Nick promised to give Har some wood from his plentiful stash. Although it was only eleven, they quit, famished from the fresh air and exercise.

"Why don't we see what the Crusty Café has to offer for an early lunch," Rachel said. "Maybe we could buy take-out for Har."

"Yes, let's," Ruth said. "I'm hungry enough to eat some of that driftwood."

They pulled into the restaurant parking lot next to a truck with the name of an extermination service printed in grass green. The driver, wearing a bright green billed cap, unloaded two tanks and a small air compressor from the back and wheeled them into the building.

"Ew," said Ruth and Rachel simultaneously.

"I agree," Nick said, backing out of the lot. "How about a sub instead?"

• • •

By the end of January, the light began to last longer in the afternoon, but the rain poured down almost every day. In the middle of February, though, the forecast promised three warm days without rain. Ruth and Rachel took advantage of them and rented a spool of extension cord. They rolled the cable down to the first tree they'd cut down. They set to sawing it and after a few fits and starts, they managed to cut the log into firewood lengths, taking turns with the saw.

"This is a breeze compared to sawing it by hand," Rachel said. "Maybe someday we'll graduate to cutting trees down with it." She unzipped her red sweatshirt.

"Yeah. Makes you wonder why they always made it sound like loggers had it so tough."

"Probably to keep women from doing it for a living and earning the big bucks. You ever notice how that is?"

"Oh, yeah. It's slowly coming to an end, that sort of discrimination."

"Too slowly."

They rolled the cord back onto the reel and then moved it to the next tree. By the time they'd hauled it to the tree by the creek, they were panting.

Ruth said, "I'm pooped. Let's take a break." She opened her pink fleece anorak.

"Yes, let's."

Ruth leaned against a tree. "Oh, no," she said, peering down the hill. "Trouble."

A bearded man stumped his way uphill, sticking close to the top of the creek bank. He was dressed in factory-fresh denim and carried a walking stick he was using to whack his way through the underbrush. He nodded when he saw them, struggling their way.

"Run and hide?" asked Rachel.

Ruth shook her head. She ground her right fist into her left palm.

"Drown him in the creek?"

Ruth frowned. "Maybe as a last resort."

"Damn," Rachel murmured, becoming pale. "I ... I thought we'd have till April. Too bad we can't just dump a tree on him."

There was no time to reply, because the man had reached them. He leaned on his stick and stood, catching his breath. Ruth mentally composed an apology and wondered if she had enough money in her bank account for bail. Sweat trickled down her back. She glanced at Rachel, who nervously swayed from foot to foot, like a little girl about to pee her pants.

"I think I may be trespassing," the man said. "I've been following the creek for at least an hour, hoping to get to a road, so I don't have to clamber back down through all that brush."

A huge breath escaped from Ruth. "You don't, ah, live around here?"

"No. We're visiting some of my wife's relatives in Crusty Beach. We come from Kansas. Is this public land?"

Rachel smiled at him. "No, it's all privately owned. We own all of it. All the way down to the road. And some on the other side of it. In Crusty Beach too."

Ruth mentally groaned, wishing Rachel would quit babbling before she gave any secrets away.

"Oh, I'm sorry."

"That's all right," Ruth jumped in. "No harm done. Just follow the creek up the hill and you'll soon go by our houses. At the highway, take a right and it'll take you down to Crusty in no time."

The man left, taking long strides, his crisp denim swishing with each step.

Ruth said, "Sons-a-bitch! I almost crapped my pants." She pushed her hair behind her ears.

"I couldn't stop talking. It felt like my mouth was on automatic fabrication, like a politician's."

They laughed shakily.

Rachel groaned and rubbed her back. "We'll *have* to rent the ATV as soon as possible. And cover up the sawdust and woodchips with pine needles."

"I don't think the owners will notice."

"No, not if we're careful."

"Then next year we can start earlier and dump a few more."

Chapter 19

NICK CAME DOWN WITH the flu. He ran a high fever and coughed so violently that Rachel feared he might have pneumonia. The coughing stage passed quickly, but it was followed by a runny nose so severe that he had scabs from wiping it. By some stroke of good fortune, Rachel didn't catch it. It was the day she turned the calendar to March before Nick was finally well enough to walk to the mailbox.

He came back with more mail than usual, mostly birthday cards for her. He panted, winded from the short walk. "Har put up another Virgin carving by the mailboxes. This one has a big, toothy grin. Looks a lot like Bill Clinton."

Rachel chuckled. "You should come with me next time I visit Ruth. My favorite Virgin is the crabbiest-looking dame imaginable."

"I'll have to see that. I finally met that Vivian. She looks like an aging hooker!"

"Doesn't she though."

He sat down at the breakfast bar, drinking the tea

she poured for him. "Using that much makeup must cause a huge carbon footprint."

Rachel laughed. "Ruth will get a charge out of that. Say, what do you think about cutting down a couple of those trees on the west side of the house? Just enough to see the ocean a little better?"

"I'd hate to lose the trees. Those Sitka's must be two hundred feet tall." He stirred a scant teaspoon of sugar into his tea.

"We wouldn't cut all of them, just two or three."

"They'll fall soon enough. Or get diseased. Let's leave them until then."

She kept quiet. She'd wait a couple of years and then cut them down. He'd probably never even notice.

• • •

The girls called to wish her a happy birthday and catch up on the news. They didn't seem hugely interested in what Rachel had to say, so she let them jabber on about their lives. They spoke to Nick for a few minutes but soon ran out of conversation. She'd been the parent they'd spoken with the most when they were growing up, and it had remained so.

Being forty-one gave her mixed feelings. She still felt young, but she was living the life of a much older woman. Since both she and Nick were retired, they lived quietly. Nick puttered around the greenhouse with his plants, and she sewed quilts. They didn't go out in the evenings, and they went to bed early, usually after a quiet evening of television. It certainly was a leisurely life.

Rachel knew that only a few lucky people could do mostly as they chose and weren't compelled to slave away until they were in their sixties. Being dissatisfied about it made her feel undeserving and spoiled. But with the continual rains, she became lethally bored. Except, that is, when she and Ruth worked on their logging project. Then, she felt young and daring, which was probably why she liked Ruth so much.

She put her birthday cards in a shoebox, ordered two jars of Visible Difference face cream, and bought a Barbie doll to sew evening gowns for, something that she'd always wanted to do and finally had time for. She shoved age out of her mind, shut the curtains in her nook to block out the rain, and using some soup cans for weights, began to exercise her arms. The beginning of flabby bat wings had appeared, and she was determined to keep them at bay for at least another decade.

• • •

Vivian stopped in for coffee late one sunny morning when Rachel was scratching around in a flower bed. "I finally have time to visit now that Dusty's back at school."

Rachel stood up and brushed the soil from her oldest jeans. "Let's go in then." It was close to lunchtime, and she had a kettle of stew simmering on the stove. The polite thing would be to invite the woman to eat with them, but Rachel didn't much care for her. She put cups of coffee on the dining table.

"Do you take sugar or milk or anything?"

"No, black's fine."

Vivian's beady eyes darted around the house, clearly assessing the value of all she could see. Her perfume, a cheap musk that smelled like candle wax mixed with urine, oozed its smelly way across the table. Rachel cracked open the window.

"Nice to have sunny weather for a change," she said. "I really love working outside when it's like this." She hoped the woman would take the hint.

"It makes *me* feel like seeing people. I hate going anywhere when it's rainy, being as how everyone's gloomy then."

She nodded, waiting for the woman to come to the point of her visit, if there was one.

"You got it fixed up real cute in here."

"I wish we could afford a little more furniture."

"Just charge it."

"Ah, no."

Vivian giggled. "My cards are maxed out too."

Rachel didn't correct her, wishing she'd finish her coffee and leave before Nick came in from the greenhouse for lunch.

But luck was not with her. He entered the house, and before he spotted the women, he sang out, "Lunch ready? I'm so hungry I could eat some of Ruth's driftwood."

There was no help for it; Rachel had to invite Vivian to eat with them. She kept it simple, with only cheese and crackers accompanying the stew. And she used the oldest dishes, something Nick noticed and raised his eyebrows about. She ignored him and plunked the kettle onto the table on top of a dingy potholder that had been overlooked when she'd bleached the grungy dish towels.

They sat down, and Rachel asked Nick, "Are any more of your seeds up?"

"Besides the lettuce, just cucumbers and parsley. We'll be eating salads within a couple weeks if the lettuce keeps growing like it is."

"Oh, in your greenhouse. I wisht I had one. Food is so expensive, and Dusty eats so much." Vivian sighed and took another ladle of stew.

"If we get extra, we'll bring it over for you," said Nick. "But I don't imagine your boy cares much for salads and veggies."

"No, not scarcely. He'd rather have stuff that's deep fried."

"Yeah, our girls went through that, but practically overnight, as soon as they got interested in boys, they started watching their weight and ate next to nothing," Rachel said.

She ate little, irritation stealing her appetite. Nick didn't eat much either.

When Vivian left the table to use the bathroom, Rachel noticed that she'd lost a little weight. Was it deliberate? She was overcome with guilt about serving such a spartan lunch. She'd be *kind* and offer the woman dessert. Yes. She probably didn't get many treats, and she would serve her a dish of ice cream. With fudge sauce. And peanuts. Topped with a huge blob of whipped cream. She'd practice a little 'Minnesota Nice' before she forgot how.

Chapter 20

RUTH TOOK THE 150-mile trip to Newport in early March. All the way there, she regretted not asking Rachel to come along for company. She stopped at a large shopping mall where she stocked up on vitamins, lotions, and cosmetics that weren't available in Crusty Beach. Then she got some navy blue uniform shirts for Har, the only color he ever wore.

Her second stop was at a small, cheery shop that sold needlework kits and supplies. The best sales on latch hook kits were held at this time of year, and she happily spent two hours digging through the jam-packed merchandise, trying to decide which kits to purchase. One, a scenic design of an eagle flying high over a mountain with a forest in the foreground, reminded her of Oregon. She snatched it up, planning to eliminate the eagle and fill the background with sky and glimpses of the ocean. She laughed out loud as she selected several shades of blue, pre-cut yarn, thinking that Rachel would love the rug, perhaps even use it as a wall hanging. It was the perfect gift of a priceless memory.

Lastly, she went to her favorite store, a paperback exchange, where she browsed until closing time, selecting books she wanted to read. She bought only a handful of new books by her very favorite writers each year. For the rest, secondhand paperbacks suited her just fine.

After she'd driven halfway back to Crusty Beach, she was tempted to pull into a motel for the night. Instead, she bought a large cup of coffee and ambled around the lot of a fast-food restaurant. She bought a candy bar and nibbled on it slowly while she drove. When she turned into her driveway, she was exhausted. She'd definitely ask Rachel to accompany her next time.

• • •

The next week, while Nick took an excursion boat trip up the Rogue River, she and Rachel rented the ATV and hauled the firewood. They kept a nervous eye out for hikers while they loaded the trailer, but no one interrupted their task. It was late afternoon when they finished hauling the wood, and after dumping the last load outside of the woodshed, Rachel plunked down on the tailgate. Ruth sank onto the chopping block.

"I know I should drive this back before the rental place closes, but I'm too tired to go," said Rachel. "I'll just pay for an extra day. It's not *that* much."

Ruth said, "I'm tired too. I ache everywhere."

"How about a sauna? Nick finally got it done."

"Yes!"

Rachel said, "Have you ever been in one of those electric ones?"

"Yes. They're not *quite* as good as the traditional ones, but I'm so sore that I don't give a damn."

"Ok, come over in about an hour and a half. It'll be hot enough by then." Rachel got up from the trailer and plodded stiffly home.

After Ruth heated some leftovers for their supper, she packed clean clothes and her favorite shampoo into a shopping bag and walked over to Rachel's.

"It's about one-hundred-seventy," Rachel said. "Is that warm enough for you?"

"Sounds perfect. I haven't been in one for so long, any warmer would probably be too hot."

Relaxing in the steam room with its spotless cedar paneling gradually eased Ruth's aches and pains. She showered, scrubbing with the long-handled, natural-bristle brush she'd brought along. After she finished, she stretched out on the bench in the dressing room to rest for a few minutes.

She jerked awake and peered at her watch, which she'd placed on a table covered with various bath products. Only twenty minutes had passed, but she felt as refreshed as if she'd slept for hours. Her skin was silky smooth from the exfoliation. She stepped into the breezeway and went to the service door, which stood open to the warm evening.

"I'm done, and I feel great!" She spoke loudly but didn't enter the house.

Rachel stepped out of the nook with a smile. "You'll have to come again. Want an ice-cold beer?"

As good as it would taste, Ruth was tired and Rachel looked dragged out too. "I think not. All I want to do is go home and read in bed till I fall asleep. Thanks *so* much."

The sun was low in the sky and Ruth reminded herself to set the clocks ahead tomorrow, glad to welcome the longer evenings. Even though she knew enough to expect a good share of rainy days in March, it was better than northern Minnesota, where the ground was still covered with two feet of snow.

Chapter 21

RACHEL TOOK AN APPLE from her jacket pocket and polished it on her taupe jeans. She bit into it, dividing her attention between the ocean and Nick, who was looking for agates. The tart crispness of the fruit made her wish for more, since the fresh breeze and the ever-changing ocean exhilarated her, increasing her appetite. She took one last bite and flung the core into the ocean, wondering if throwing vegetable matter into the water could be considered littering. She thought not. While chewing the apple, she slipped her tongue into a new hollow, which contained only a portion of the tooth. Instantly she spit the chewed-up apple into the palm of her hand, desperately searching for the porcelain crown.

It wasn't there.

Damn.

She kicked her shoes off and charged into the water where she saw the apple core bobbing. The waves were gentle, but the water felt like ice. She sloshed through it rapidly and grabbed the core, then sped to shore, her feet and lower legs so cold they ached. Luckily, the crown was embedded in the apple. She pulled it out and held it in her mouth while she squeezed water from her pants and slipped into her shoes. Then she jogged up the shore to Nick.

"We're going to have to go into Crusty right away." She held the crown up near her mouth and smiled. "We should be able to catch the dentist before he leaves."

Nick looked at her and chuckled. "Cute," he said.

They did get to the dentist's office in time. It was located on the second floor of the bank building, had dark paneling and old-fashioned, golden oak cabinets. The dentist looked about twenty, and he was making an attempt to grow a beard, though his youthful effort seemed like it could use a little fertilizer. Rachel fervently hoped that she wasn't his very first patient.

After examining her, Dr. Beckford said, "There's quite a bit of decay on the remaining tooth, and after I remove it, there won't be enough left to hold onto the crown. It'll probably fall off the first time you bite into something."

"So, what do we do?"

"You'll need a bridge. I'll have to extract the root of that bicuspid. You'll need a longer appointment to have the adjacent two teeth prepped for the bridge."

"How long will I be without teeth?" she asked, rubbing her elbow.

"About six to eight weeks. My assistant has gone for the day, but I should be able to extract that tooth now, so the healing process can begin."

Resigning herself to spending the next two months mostly at home, she said, "Dig out your pliers." At least by the time summer arrived, she'd have teeth.

Dr. Beckford paused from filling a tray with the ominous looking instruments of his trade. "Do you have any dental insurance?"

"I'm not certain. We do have both the medical and eye-care insurance that was part of my husband's retirement package, but I don't know about the dental. I *think* we have it."

"The bridge is expensive. If you don't have insurance, you'll have to pay at least half of it to cover lab expenses. Credit cards are okay."

Rachel supposed it was necessary to pay ahead of time, especially since she was new to the area. "Okay. It's certainly something I must have."

• • •

While she was waiting for her bridge, she saw only Nick, Ruth, and her dentist. She did her grocery shopping early in the morning and forced Nick to come with her to write the checks and do the required socializing.

She was nearly out of Shalimar, but rather than going into the drugstore, she ordered a large bottle of cologne and a small bottle of perfume. They were costly, so she resisted the matching bath products. Financially, as long as no other emergencies landed on them, they'd be fine. But in idle moments she worried and checked the newspaper for jobs.

They purchased white paint for the exterior of the cabin, and spring green for the trim. Rachel scraped and painted the walls, rather than hiring someone, because their dental plan *had* been cancelled, and her bridge was ridiculously expensive. On the increasingly prevalent sunny days, she worked away in solitude, listening to the birds sing.

Har often walked by on the trail that roughly followed the stream, but he never said a word or even more than glanced at her. He was similar in build to Nick, with light brown hair and eyes that were a tropical-looking greenish blue. He never smiled. Rachel worried that Nick might suffer a similar stroke, leaving him without speech or worse. So far, though, he'd been lucky. Even his limp had vanished.

Ruth helped her paint the trim. They also painted the interior of the porch with the leftover green paint. After they finished, Rachel heated water for tea, which they drank in the porch, sitting on a long bench positioned in front of the screened west wall.

"Have you found a renter for the place?" Ruth asked.

"I haven't advertised yet. I didn't know when I'd be done painting and cleaning it."

"I may have someone for you, although it would only be from the first of June to the end of August. My boss's nephew, Ben Larkin, is looking for a quiet place to live while he compiles a cookbook from his grandmother's recipes. He teaches high school English."

"Teachers are usually trustworthy. Can you get me his number?" She'd *probably* have her teeth before he arrived. She was tired of carefully chewing on her left side to preserve the temporary caps covering the two ground-off teeth on the right side. And, she was weary of not feeling confident enough to talk to more people. Only three weeks, maybe two, if she were lucky, and she'd have them.

"Yes, as soon as I get it from his aunt."

Rachel finished her tea and asked, "Could you put a few streaks of blonde in my hair? It's getting so dingy."

"Sure," Ruth said. "I did it every year for a friend of mine in Minnesota and it always came out nice. Just get one of those kits."

"I already did, but Nick refuses to help."

"Men."

They had a second cup of tea, listening to the gentle wind blowing through the branches of the evergreen trees. The stream, much lower now, made a gentle burble, rather than the jarring roar it had produced for most of the winter.

Ruth dropped her loafers onto the floor and wiggled her stocking-clad feet in a patch of sunlight.

"I thought it was up here," said a woman, in a rather whiney voice. "I'm getting tired of looking for it."

They both snapped to attention, looking out the window, but they couldn't see anyone.

"So am I," answered a male. "I spent a good two hours carving our initials into that heart."

"Maybe bark grew back over it."

"I doubt it."

The voices were coming closer. Ruth and Rachel glanced at each other in alarm and dropped to their knees, peering over the windowsill, certain the couple owned the land they'd logged, but no one was visible.

Rachel whispered, "I don't remember seeing any trees with hearts carved on them. Do you?"

"I'd never have cut them down if I'd seen carving on them," she murmured, adding, "They're getting close. Sons-a-bitch!"

The young couple came into view, searching the tree trunks. The man scratched his head and said, "It's like it got up and walked away."

"That's dumb! I think it was aliens that took it."

"They must've, cause it's not here."

Rachel shook with silent laughter.

Ruth giggled, and they crawled to the door and into the cabin. They eased the door shut and sprawled on the floor, convulsed with stifled laughter.

Finally, Ruth said, "I wonder how much we could log off before they actually noticed."

Rachel grinned, "If those two are the owners, probably close to clear-cut."

Chapter 22

VIVIAN OPENED HER MAILBOX to discover a huge bag of lettuce leaves behind the bills. It was the third time Nick and Rachel had put some there, and it was delicious, though she'd grown tired of washing each leaf before she ate it.

Dusty loathed salads, not that she saw much of him anymore. After he'd gotten his driver's license, he'd nabbed a part-time job bagging groceries in Brookings. When he *was* home, he slept a few hours and spent all of his limited time on studying and managed to keep his grades up. Vivian missed him and knew her days as a parent were nearly over. At this time next year, he'd graduate and move out. And that would be the end of the support checks.

She stepped into the house, her stomach churning from anxiety. She had one year to find someone, preferably a boyfriend who'd give her a stake to make her Las Vegas dream come true. Or maybe catch a husband, one with enough money to get her out of this rickety trailer before it collapsed like a crumpled beer can.

She piled the bills onto the counter and emptied the bag of lettuce into the sink. Looking down, she was disgusted that the roll of fat above her waist wasn't melting away fast enough. And Vivian was hungry, her stomach snarling to be fed, so she stood at the sink and rinsed the lettuce, gnawing the leaves without dressing until she grew tired of chewing.

• • •

The last day in May she began to take walks in an effort to rid herself of the pounds. A car stopped beside her.

"I'm looking for the Christensons." The speaker was an attractive man in his early forties. He wore a pair of light driving gloves, so she couldn't tell if he was wearing a wedding band.

Just in case, she flashed him a huge smile and sucked in her stomach. "The first house on the right from here. Are you one of their relatives?"

"No, I'm renting their guest cottage for the summer."

"Oh." She thrust her ample bosom into his face until the magenta of her T-shirt reflected off his cheeks.

He shrank back into his car.

"Seeing as how I live across the road from them, maybe we'll get to know each other. I'm Vivian Snell."

"Yes, maybe. I'm Benjamin Larkin." He looked a little disconcerted, but he smiled weakly and drove away.

His car looked brand new, and he'd been dressed in a dark tan safari jacket and slacks that looked like they cost a lot of bucks. With any luck, she could snap him up. But he had a high-class look, and that type usually preferred women who were less flamboyant than she was. If she wanted him, she'd have to tone down.

Thinking about that helped her walk for a full hour. For fifty seconds of it she jogged until her heart lurched wildly behind her ribs, as if it were a wild bird trying to escape from a cage, so she dropped back to a walk. No point in *killing* herself for a man.

• • •

With all the unaccustomed hours alone, she did some exercises, hoping to flatten her stomach. And, she pored over all the women's magazines in search of an updated hairstyle. Torn between having a shorter do, which was suggested for women her age, and leaving it long because men liked it, she gave the choice to her hairdresser. She left the shop with medium ash-brown hair brushing her shoulders. Although she feared it wouldn't attract attention, it *did* make her look youthful, so she kept it.

Whenever she picked up her mail, she began to check Rachel's mailbox for letters to their tenant, hoping he hadn't rented a box at the post office downtown. One day she was rewarded with a fat manila envelope with the name, Benjamin Larkin, on it, in care of the Christensons. She tucked it into a beauty magazine and smuggled it into her house.

The envelope had its metal tabs bent over, but the seal hadn't been moistened. Vivian tipped about a dozen letters onto the table. She shoved the bills and business letters back into the manila envelope, ran across the road, and stuck it into Rachel's mailbox.

She'd kept the single personal letter from a woman named Sheila, hoping to find out more about Ben before she sunk her claws into him. That she'd committed a federal offense by swiping the letter didn't bother her in the least. What did irk her was that it was time for her to leave for work, and she had to postpone reading it until she got home.

Chapter 23

BY THE TIME BEN showed up, Rachel had her dental bridge cemented in place and one of the box springs and mattresses from the house installed in the cottage. She welcomed the interesting man wholeheartedly. He was a high school English teacher, but even though his vocabulary was probably vast, he spoke naturally rather than try to impress people with his knowledge.

Nick liked him too. They all went to the beach twice, once taking Ruth along. Ben took them to lunch, but not to the Crusty Café, about which they had warned him. Most of the time, though, he seemingly preferred to work in solitude.

The summer was colder than normal, so Nick advertised for a secondhand wood stove and found a lady outside of Crusty Beach who wanted to sell her Franklin stove. The price was right, although they had to buy a new grate. Ben and Nick hauled some firewood from the stockpile in the garage to burn at the cottage when the nights were chilly. The men spent a day installing an expensive, insulated stovepipe, which cut the risk of fire.

While they were putting it in the living area of the cottage, Rachel walked down and brought Ben a wool blanket, draping it over the back of one of the kitchen chairs. Though he'd only been in the cottage for a short time, he already had stacks of recipes organized on the table, all labeled and clipped together. His computer and a printer were set up on a battered desk by the door.

"Do you need Internet service?" Rachel asked. "We *can* get a phone in here."

Ben closed his clear blue eyes and shook his head vigorously. "No! I'm just using it to write with. I'd be too tempted to surf if I went online."

"Well, if you need one, use ours."

"I'll remember that." He hesitated, then said, "One of the neighbors is getting to be a bit of a pest. Vivian Snell. She shows up almost every morning, and it breaks my concentration."

Rachel glanced at the windows and French doors that lined the wall opening into the screened porch. "I see. She can easily peek in to check if you're home. I'll make some curtains—maybe café style—so you won't lose all the light.

"Thank you. I tried pulling the shades, but it made it so dark in here, I got drowsy."

Rachel took some measurements and left. At home, she quickly paged through a mail-order catalogue, but didn't find anything appealing, so she called Ruth.

"Would you like to go to Brookings with me tomorrow or the next day? I have to get some fabric to make more curtains for the cottage."

"Oh?"

"Vivian's been bothering Ben, looking through the porch windows to see if he's home. I only made valances for the public rooms."

"She loses her support checks in less than a year, so I imagine she's going after him."

"Yeah, I suppose." Rachel paused briefly. "Nick had better not die until we pay off this house, or I'll have to sell out, and I don't want to move. If I'd have known about that pension cut, I'd have insisted we buy a house we could have paid for completely."

"I'm in the same situation, even though the house is mine. I'm holding my breath until I'm old enough to get Social Security. With that and Har's life insurance, I'll have enough to live on if he should die before I do."

"I'd have to get a job, but there's not anything around here that calls for my qualifications."

"And the pay is lousy, especially for women."

"I noticed."

"Tomorrow sounds good for shopping," Ruth said. "Let's make a day of it. We can burrow around in some shops and have something for lunch that we haven't had to cook."

"Is eight too early to leave?"

• • •

In Brookings, Rachel found some floor-length curtains on a good sale. She estimated that she'd be able to cut two curtains from each fern-printed panel, so she purchased them, along with café rods.

Ruth bought some jeans in a size larger than she usually wore. "I *always* go up one size during the winter, and I'm not going to stuff myself into size tens. It makes me look fatter."

They lazily made their way to Rachel's truck, enjoying the sun and warm temperature in Brookings.

"I do that too," Rachel said. "Once in a while, I get skinny enough to fit in my eights, but with each passing year, I have more trouble losing weight." She unlocked the camper door, and they tossed their packages inside. They went north, taking the Pacific Coast Highway.

They drove along, occasionally commenting on the scenery, but decided to pass by Crusty Beach and go on to Port Orford, a place neither woman had been and both wanted to explore.

"There's supposed to be a little shop that sells prize-winning, tie-dyed T-shirts," Ruth said. "Not that I really need any clothes."

"I don't either, but something new always gives me a lift." While driving along, Rachel said, "Don't ever tell anyone this, but when I was sorting stuff to take to Oregon, I got rid of fifty-one pairs of jeans. And twenty-nine bras. I'll *never* buy and hoard like that again."

Ruth asked, "Were you poor when you were a kid?"

"I came from a large, working-class family. I was the oldest, and yes, we were rather poor."

"Well, hell, you just overcompensated a little. Are your parents still alive?"

"My mother is. She remarried before Dad was cold. After all, she needed to feed six kids. Then I had a stepfather who was a drunk, though he did make more money than my father had. I was a senior when that happened, and I left right after graduation, working my way through college. How about you?"

"I have one brother, and my parents were well off. They left their retirement home in Florida to my brother, and I got cash."

Rachel said, "And we both have husbands who worked in management in the mines. We're better off than many women."

"Indeed we are."

• • •

In Port Orford, they poked around in antique stores, a bookshop, and the shop selling T-shirts. Ruth bought a T-shirt with aqua and purple swirls, and Rachel purchased one with splotches of navy and red. After a leisurely lunch, they drove all the way to Coos Bay before heading back home. Since it was mid-week, the traffic was minimal. Still, Rachel wished they could stay overnight at an ocean-side motel, because she had cramps and felt more tired that usual.

"I don't miss them one bit," Ruth said.

"When did you go through the change?"

"When I was forty-seven. Three years ago. Before that, I was always anemic. I was amazed at how much more energy I had after I was done with the cursed thing."

"Something to look forward to. How about hot flashes?"

"I never had one. Finns aren't especially prone to them, thanks to Genghis Kahn and his raiders. They gave us Asian DNA to avoid them.

"My mother never had any, so I guess there's a good chance I won't either." Rachel yawned. "Keep an eye open for a drive-in. I need some coffee. You want to drive for a while?"

They were on the outskirts of Crusty Beach when Rachel asked, "Is Ben married? He doesn't wear a ring, but not everyone does."

"I'm quite certain he is. I remember my boss mentioning that his wife is an invalid. He never talks about his personal life."

"No, he doesn't."

They got home around eight and Rachel helped Ruth haul in her purchases. Rachel decided to leave hers in the truck until morning, since she felt so cruddy.

• • •

Nick had made a pasta salad, and she had a small bowl while they discussed the trip. He said, "Must be the weather or something, because I'm tired and I didn't do that much."

He took a quick shower and went to bed, while Rachel filled the garden tub and soaked in lilac-scented bubbles. She dried off and walked through a light spray of Shalimar cologne. Oddly enough, the matching bottle of perfume wasn't on her sink vanity where she'd left it. She looked around, moving jars and digging into the medicine cabinet, but she couldn't find it. Could she have the symptoms of early dementia? She blocked the terrifying thought. Making a mental note to search for it in the morning, she slipped into her white cotton nightgown and crawled into bed. Nick had gone right to sleep, so Rachel stayed with him. She drank a small cup of tea and took an ibuprofen for her cramps, then turned off the light. As tired as she was, sleep didn't come immediately, since it felt peculiar to go to bed when it was still twilight outside.

It didn't bother Nick, though. He didn't toss and turn or even snore. She checked to see if he was breathing, then burrowed a hole into her pillow, stretched her feet to the cool reaches of the fresh butter-yellow sheets, and drifted off.

Chapter 24

RUTH DUMPED HER PURCHASES on the kitchen counter and dug through the refrigerator, looking for something quick to eat. Har had left one of the meatloaf sandwiches she'd prepared for him early this morning. She added mustard and onions and gobbled it down. The house seemed a little stuffy, so she walked around and opened a few windows. While she was doing that, Har came in and went directly upstairs to the room he'd slept in since living here. He walked around, flushed the toilet, and then there was silence. He always retired around nine, whether it was dark or not.

Not ready to go to bed yet, Ruth sat in her recliner with a small goblet of red wine and turned the television on, keeping the volume low while she waited for the news.

She woke with a jerk after midnight. An emergency vehicle, its siren assaulting the peaceful night, drove past her house. She stood up and stumbled to the door, her coordination clumsy from sleep. The ambulance turned into Rachel's driveway.

Dread turned Ruth cold. She nuked some old coffee and filled a thermos mug, then grabbed her purse and a flashlight. She galloped down her driveway and sped to Rachel's house. They were loading Nick into the ambulance.

Rachel stood on the porch, wearing a robe and slippers.

"Where are they taking him?" Ruth asked.

"Gold Beach."

"How is he?"

"He woke up and had trouble talking and could hardly walk. It's the worst one he's had."

"You want me to drive you? Throw some clothes on and I'll make coffee."

"Thank you." Rachel looked her over. "I'll drive, but please come with me. You hadn't been to bed yet?"

"I fell asleep in front of the TV."

Ruth brewed the coffee and filled a thermos, then smeared some crackers with peanut butter and stuffed them into a sandwich bag. Rachel came into the kitchen dressed in jeans and a navy polo shirt, brushing her chin-length, blonde hair into place. She grabbed the keys and her wallet from the counter, locked the house, and they left.

Gold Beach was about twenty miles south of Crusty Beach, and although there was fog, it wasn't very thick, so they made reasonably good time. At the hospital, Rachel hurried into the emergency room.

Ruth went to the waiting room. She was the only person there, and she pawed through the ragged magazines for something to read. It might be a long time before Rachel came out. She leaned back to skim through a story about the sex life of octogenarians, wondering whether the young writer was full of shit or serious. After reading the story, she decided he was serious but naively hopeful about the prospect of his own sex life when he grew old. She chuckled quietly.

Rachel came out after about an hour. “He’s stable. He’s speaking, though with a slur. We might as well go home.”

“Are you sure?”

“Yes. I’ve been through this three times already,” she said, weariness flattening her voice.

Ruth drove while Rachel drank coffee and ate some of the crackers.

“Have you had a chance to see a lawyer to draw up the papers for your power of attorney yet?”

“No. But I’m not procrastinating anymore. Not after tonight. As soon as he comes home, I’m insisting that we do it.”

“Good,” Ruth said. “It’s a lot easier to get it done if Nick’s lucid and agreeable to it.” The fog had become thicker and she slowed to a crawl.

“I just hope he doesn’t die. Besides missing him, well, I can’t afford it. Not yet.”

“There are options.”

“What do you mean?” Rachel asked.

“I don’t want to go into that right now. But soon I will. Probably.”

“It sounds mysterious.”

“It is.” Ruth chuckled and drove on, concentrating on staying between the fog lines.

Chapter 25

EARLY THE NEXT MORNING Vivian walked to the Christensons' and pounded repeatedly on their door, morbidly curious about the ambulance that had torn her from sleep the night before. Rachel opened the door wearing a nightgown; her hair was snarled and she had dark circles under her eyes. The ambulance must have been for Nick.

"Sleeping in?" Vivian asked, pretending she didn't know a thing about the previous night's excitement.

"Umm."

"I need to talk to Ben. Is he still renting from you guys?"

"Yeah, but he's been driving up the coast and staying wherever he lands at bedtime."

The woman didn't invite her in, even though she'd always been friendly before. "Is everything all right? You look a little under the weather." *She looks like shit.*

"No, it's not. Nick had another stroke last night and he's in the hospital."

Rachel tried to pull the door shut, but Vivian held it

open and said, "I'm sorry. I hope he's okay. Will you call me when Ben gets back?"

"I'll tell him you're looking for him." She yawned and rubbed her eyes, so Vivian left. Rachel looked like she'd been on a three-day bender.

It dawned on her, then, that since Nick had suffered a stroke, there might not be any more free lettuce in the mailbox. Not unless Rachel took over the job of watering the plants, which, according to Nick, she had no interest in doing. Vivian had finally lost enough weight to wedge herself into a pair of size twelve pants. Now she'd have to *buy* lettuce, and it wouldn't taste nearly as good as what she'd been eating free of charge.

She was nearly to her house when it struck her that she might as well get some lettuce right now, before it dried up. Rachel had no doubt climbed back into bed and fallen asleep, so Vivian simply walked across the yard and on into the greenhouse. The sturdy building was clad with siding three feet up from the ground and the rest was covered with slightly scratched Plexiglas. She knew several people who had greenhouses, but they all had covered them with plastic sheeting. A dart of envy went through her at Rachel's good fortune.

There was no lock on the door; the tables were covered with pots and deep plastic troughs planted with a variety of vegetables, but she wanted only lettuce. She twisted off leaves from numerous plants and stuffed then into an empty planting box and left. She didn't plan on coming back. In a week the plants would be dead. Nick might be dead too. Then Rachel would no longer get to spend the generous pension that Nick received. *Ha!*

• • •

At work that day, she tried to figure out something that would draw her and Ben together. He taught English and had stacks of books, mostly reference, in his cottage. The last novel she'd read had been in twelfth grade, when they'd been forced to read *Silas Marner*. She had not, in fact, read it; instead she begged a friend to fill her in on the plot. Unless it was a magazine article about beauty, glamour, sex tips, or romance, reading put her to sleep.

She mixed some tarter sauce, knowing the proportions by heart. Maybe she could write a cookbook like Ben was doing. She had quite a few good recipes, all tested on her son and his friends. And just because Ben's grandmother had made Lord Baltimore cakes regularly didn't mean it was the only recipe for a good dessert. She recalled the graham crackers she'd spread with lemon-pie filling and topped with marshmallow crème. Dusty had gobbled them down, and they were certainly easier to make than the Baltimore cake. And how about that French-style dressing she made from tomato soup? It was cheap and no one refused to eat it, even with the slight metallic taste from the can. And what about the bar recipe that called for two cups of expensive walnuts? She always substituted crushed pretzels and the bars still tasted okay.

She could work on Dusty's computer. Although she'd used it only occasionally, she knew enough about word processing to write her book on it. The spelling and grammar check should take care of all those boring rules she'd never learned. It might even be a little fun, now that she was alone so much of the time.

Mostly, though, it would give her and Ben something in common. She imagined the two of them living together, drinking screwdrivers while they pecked out recipes for money. What a *pleasant* way to make a living!

Chapter 26

RACHEL SHUT THE DOOR on Vivian and shuffled back to her bedroom, stopping in the master bath for an ibuprofen to relieve both her cramps and headache. From one of her bedroom windows she was startled to see Vivian open the door of the greenhouse and slip in. *What on earth is she doing in there?* She came out after a few minutes, carrying a seed flat heaped with something green, lettuce most likely. And she didn't sneak away but strode boldly across the yard, as if she owned the place.

After she disappeared from view, Rachel went back to bed and pulled the blankets over her. But tired as she was, she couldn't get back to sleep. There was very little of value in the greenhouse, and while she didn't mind *giving* Vivian salad greens, she minded very much that the woman stole them. *Will her behavior escalate*? Rachel instantly decided to become more vigilant about locking her doors. Also, she would buy a sturdy lock for the greenhouse.

Try as she might, she couldn't get back to sleep. Vivian's sneaking around had robbed her of sleep, so she got up and made coffee and toast. It was far too early to know if Nick would be released today or tomorrow, but from experience she doubted he'd be hospitalized any longer than that. Because she hadn't been startled awake by any phone calls giving her news of a dire nature, she assumed that Nick hadn't taken a turn for the worse. An uneasy intuition, however, told her that this stroke was more serious, and she considered calling her daughters.

No. They'd already be at work. Living three time zones from them frustrated her at times. She thought about talking with Ruth, but had a hunch that she might still be sleeping, unless Vivian had woken her too.

After she choked down her breakfast, she went into the bathroom to look for her bottle of Shalimar perfume, even searching in Nick's vanity, but it was nowhere to be found. She also discovered that her spare jar of Visible Difference had vanished. There was no doubt in her mind what happened to it. Vivian had simply helped herself.

To use up some time until she called Ruth, she stripped the linens off the bed and made it up with rose-printed ones. Then she showered with water as hot as was comfortable, hoping to ease the tension in her muscles. She'd just slipped into her robe when the phone rang.

"Have you heard anything?" Ruth asked.

"Not yet. I'm calling the hospital in about an hour." She told Ruth about her missing cosmetics and her suspicions about Vivian taking them.

Ruth said, "She *is* light-fingered. It's a good idea to pick up your mail as soon as it's delivered; I've seen her digging through my box once or twice."

"Oh, great. Ben said one of his colleagues had sent a personal letter along with his bills, but he never got it. I wonder if she had anything to do with it vanishing."

"It's entirely possible. Call me as soon as you hear about Nick."

"I will," Rachel said. "Thanks so much for being with me last night."

"Anytime."

• • •

She dressed in jeans and a pale blue blouse that Nick was especially fond of when she visited him that afternoon. He had a slight but distinctive slur in his speech, and she had to listen closely to understand what he said. The nurse who checked his vitals found it difficult to understand *her* rapid, Iron Range dialect, and nearly *impossible* to comprehend what Nick was saying.

What Rachel found even more disturbing was that Nick was unable to walk without a walker, making him seem aged beyond his years. For exercise, they slowly roamed the corridor to the nurse's station, then turned and went all the way to the lobby. He showed signs of tiring, so they rested, sitting there for several minutes.

"Dr. Crawford says I'll be able to get by with a cane soon. And, I got a different blood pressure medicine, so this won't happen again." He spoke slowly and was putting on an attitude of excessive optimism, for her benefit probably. Or it might be for himself, to deny the reality.

"Good!" She said it brightly, forcing a big smile. They went back to his room and he settled in with a yawn. Promising to be back in the evening, Rachel left, stopping at the desk to find out when Dr. Crawford made his rounds. She had to talk with him.

• • •

In the small town of Gold Beach, she picked up a few groceries and bought a pair of casual sandals that were on sale. She didn't really need them, but the price was so low that she couldn't resist. She kept shopping, buying inexpensive items to push back the apprehension that kept taking little nips at her guts.

An ad for a garage sale was tacked up, so she drove a mile out of town. The lady was selling piles of fabric from her mother's quilting stash.

"I wish I'd learned to sew," said the stout lady holding the sale. "Mother never could get me interested. I'm the only daughter, and after she died, my brothers dumped all this quilt material on me. Are my prices okay?"

She was selling fabric by the *pound*. "Yes, they're quite reasonable." Rachel kept her face placid and pleasant, hiding her greedy excitement. She mentally calculated just how much she dared spend. She chose several large pieces, a multitude of fat quarters and nine yards of material featuring huge ocean waves. After checking her watch, she reluctantly left.

Back in Gold Beach, she had a seafood salad and a cup of coffee, though she only picked at the salad. Trepidation had killed her appetite. She did, nonetheless, finish her coffee, knowing she needed to stay alert for yet another hour or two.

Finally, it was time to go back to the hospital. She managed to catch the doctor before she saw her husband. As she had suspected, Nick was worse off than he was letting on.

Dr. Crawford said, "*If* there are no problems tonight, he can go home tomorrow."

"Um, how about therapy?" As bad as a cane was, the walker made Nick seem fragile, not the strong, capable man who'd made major decisions for a large mining company. He'd suddenly become elderly, insignificant. *How does he feel?* Compassion filled her heart and tears threatened to spill. *I will not cry. I will not cry.*

"We'll discuss that when he comes in for a checkup next week. He should go to Medford for some more tests. They have a larger facility and can do more than we are able to here." He glanced at his watch, clearly in a hurry.

She nodded and stepped aside, then made her way down the corridor to Nick's room. She paused, pasting a cheerful look on her face to mask the grinding worry.

Chapter 27

"HE SENDS THE MONEY for *me*," Dusty said. "I don't see why I can't have it for a place of my own." He slouched at the kitchen table, pushing soggy cornflakes around in his bowl.

"It's against the law for a minor to live alone. I only agreed to you moving out at seventeen because the school is in Corvallis, and that's too terrible far to drive every day."

Frustrated, Vivian used all her willpower to keep from throwing dishes at him. His recent decision to go to school in Oregon rather than California was made because he disliked his stepmother and couldn't bear the thought of living with her for a measly two years.

"You treat me like I'm a baby. I've already been working for over three months and pay for all my own stuff."

He did, in fact, pay for his gas, his car insurance, and his fast food. "It's only one more year—eleven months, if you want to split hairs. If you insist on leaving now, that's fine, but *you'll have to live with your father*."

He stomped out of the house in disgust. She fully expected him to peal out of the driveway. Amazingly, he took out the lawnmower and began to cut the grass. It did need cutting, but already it had begun to get brown from the lack of rain. Then too, she had not one tree or shrub to shade her place, so it turned brown early unless she pumped water on it from the creek. This year, she'd do that again, but only on the east side of the trailer, where she had privacy from the traffic. The blue tarp was still up, giving her a little shade. Dusty had locked most of his tools in his trunk, pushing the larger ones under the house, so the area was cleaned up and almost inviting.

• • •

Dusty left for work, and Vivian settled down under the tarp in an old kitchen chair with a glass of ice water and a magazine. She studied an article that gave sure-fire methods to capture a man's interest. For the first time in her life, though, some of the advice seemed a little juvenile, and with a sinking feeling she knew she was getting old.

The weight loss had made her ass attractively smaller and her gut less prominent, but with each pound she shed, more lines were revealed on her face. They revealed her age as surely as her birth certificate did. The expensive cream she'd lifted from Rachel's bathroom minimized them wonderfully, but how could she get any more when Rachel kept her house locked all the time, even when she walked out to get the mail?

Without the cream, she looked much older than her actual age. She might as well let her hair go gray, cut it short, and have it permed in tight, immovable curls like her mother used to wear. She shuddered and went back to reading the magazine, avidly memorizing every word.

• • •

Vivian dressed in dark blue and waited until twilight. She sneaked through Rachel's yard and crossed the bridge, following the creek path to see if Ben was home. She carried a small cardboard folder holding her few recipes, along with a few notes she'd scribbled. She stepped on a stick, which snapped, making her jump, so she slowed her pace. Suddenly she spotted someone standing beside the trail.

It was Arnold Schwarzenegger.

Vivian stopped instantly, and then realized that it was merely another carving of the Virgin, though considerably larger than most. She took a few deep breaths and continued to the cottage.

Ben was sitting in the porch with a small table lamp as his only illumination. He was writing something in a notebook and wearing a beige terrycloth robe. He yawned and shoved his pencil into the spring at the top of the notebook. Clearly, he was about to retire, so she hesitated, standing in the shadows, trying to decide if she should continue to the door or go back home. She *could* ask for help with her book; being asked for advice always flattered men. If only she didn't have her crappy period, this would be the perfect time to seduce him.

He snapped off the light and stepped into his dark house, deciding the matter for her. She left, creeping quietly on the trail, past Arnold and across the bridge.

Since she was out and about, she decided to get some lettuce, so she skulked across Rachel's back yard. A couple of lights were on in the house, but there were no other signs of life. She tugged at the greenhouse door, but it wouldn't budge. The dim light showed a padlock screwed onto the door and frame, so she stomped angrily home. It was too late to drive to the grocery store, and the only other vegetables in the house were canned green beans and frozen broccoli, neither of which she much liked. But it was either them or starve because wrinkles or not, she refused to eat any more of the high-calorie food that she fed to Dusty.

Chapter 28

AS SHE'D DONE FOR the past two summers, Ruth hauled several of Har's carvings to a shop catering to the tourists. Amazingly, they sold well and for a respectable price. Ruth often puzzled over why he had chosen to carve Mary. He'd been raised in a Lutheran family and as far as she knew, he'd never even been to a wedding in a Catholic church. But he'd never told her, so it would remain a mystery.

Her work was reduced to two days a month until fall, when people used the rainy weather to pursue indoor projects. On her first day that June, there were few customers, so she cut some mats and framed two photographs. Then she dusted and tidied, merely putting in her hours until closing time. The store was quieter than usual. Her boss was struggling through the bookkeeping and as inclined to conversation as one of Har's carvings.

When Ruth got home, she felt so isolated that she called Rachel before she started supper.

"How are things going today?"

Rachel said, "Okay for me, but Nick got tired out from doing some legal business in Crusty Beach. After we ate, he went to his recliner to watch TV and he dozed off."

"Ah, you don't suppose—"

"No, I checked. He's still breathing. Why don't you come over for a glass of wine after you eat? Or maybe we'll split the bottle. I can't seem to relax."

"I'll see you in about an hour."

Ruth fried sausage and French toast, and after she and Har ate, she piled the dishes on the counter and told him where she'd be. She felt quite certain that he understood what she said, although he never gave any feedback. She grabbed a sweater from the back of her teal and brown plaid couch and left, strolling along the stone-covered path. After crossing the bridge, she went to the screen door in the breezeway, but strangely enough, it was locked. Ruth knocked and then called out, "Yoo-hoo."

Rachel stepped out of her laundry room and lifted the hook. She locked it after Ruth came in.

"I think you may be right about Vivian. Ever since we moved here, I've misplaced things like shampoo, cans of coffee and even laundry detergent." She led the way into the dining room, where a bottle of white wine and glasses sat on a freshly polished brass tray in the center of the table. "I blamed the stress of the move for screwing up my memory, but good grief, we've lived here for nearly a year. Not one single thing has vanished since I began to lock the doors."

Ruth said, "I've never had anything disappear from *inside* the house, but last week a new clothes basket I left under the line walked away."

Rachel poured glasses of wine and removed the plastic wrap from a crystal bowl of fresh strawberries. "Want some whipped cream to dip these in?"

"No, this is fine."

"We went in to see a lawyer today, giving our power of attorney to each other." She spoke quietly, even though the television likely masked their conversation.

Ruth nodded. "Good."

"I think he finally realizes that he might end up as a vegetable, but it's tough to admit that to yourself. Naturally he's depressed." She rubbed her elbow.

"You seem to be doing well."

"I forced myself to face the worst that could happen after he had his first stroke. I stayed home and cried for a day, but luckily I didn't know about his pension then, or I'd have bawled for a month." She dipped a strawberry into her wine and popped it into her mouth, chewing it with relish. "How did you cope when Har had his?"

"The same way. People think I'm tough and cold-blooded because I don't fall apart and bawl. Like you, I do my crying in private."

"Minnesota women," said Rachel with a wry smile.

Ruth chuckled quietly. She sniffed her wine and then sipped it. "This tastes good. It's not too dry."

"Yeah, it is. I hauled three cases from Minnesota, left over from the days when Nick had a glass or two with nearly every dinner."

"What's the occasion today?"

"Um ... how about friendship?"

They ate the berries and drank the wine, relaxing, and getting a bit tipsy, neither of them ever having drunk much. Both chuckled over their logging venture and planned to do more, as soon as the rains started. They had just poured the last of the bottle into their glasses when they heard something clatter onto the floor in the family room.

They stared at each other.

"Nick?" Rachel called, grasping her goblet tightly.

There was no answer.

"Nick, are you okay?" she asked more loudly.

Ruth went to Rachel and took her glass.

They walked slowly toward the family room.

Chapter 29

RACHEL STEPPED INTO THE family room, filled with dread.

Ruth walked right behind her. The remote had fallen to the floor, and Nick lay back on the recliner—maybe asleep. Rachel grabbed his wrist, checking for a pulse.

"Oh, shit," she said, placing his hand back on the arm of the chair. "I'd better try CPR."

Ruth put the glasses down on a side table. She felt his cheek and the back of his neck. "I don't think so; he's already cooling."

"You're sure?"

"Yes. Remember, I worked in health care."

"Shit." She sank down on the couch.

"He must have died earlier, some time before the remote fell."

Rachel jumped up and covered Nick with the afghan that was draped on the couch, noticing her husband seemed somehow shrunken. She sat back down at one end of the couch. Ruth handed her the glass of wine.

"I'll call 911 after a minute." She gulped the drink.

Ruth nodded and sat down on an occasional chair opposite her.

"He *could* have made the effort to linger on until the house was paid for," Rachel said, angrily.

Ruth gazed at her and nodded but said nothing.

Rachel jumped up and adjusted the afghan so it covered his lifeless hand. "Unless I get a good job or find someone rich to shack up with, I'll have to sell the house and move. Damn!" Her eyes filled with tears. "I'll miss you so much."

"There are other options," Ruth said, quietly.

"What?"

"Don't report his death and keep collecting the checks."

"I'm sure news of his death will get into the system and be picked up by his pension providers before the week is out. You know how fast it is with computers."

"No, what I mean is, don't report his death to *anyone*."

"What? Just let him rot away in his chair for a year or two?" Rachel couldn't believe they were actually having this surreal conversation. She must be having a nightmare or a hallucination.

"No, certainly not. He'll start to smell by noon. We have to get rid of the body tonight."

"It sounds like you've already done this."

Ruth paused.

"You *haven't*."

"I have. Har isn't my husband. He's my brother-in-law, Harlan. My husband, Harvey, died when Harlan was on a visit from the veteran's home in Medford." She leaned toward Rachel. "So, I buried my husband with full military honors in Medford and kept Harlan and the pension. I told everyone that he had a stroke and couldn't speak. Actually, Harlan came back from a POW camp in Vietnam like that."

Rachel scratched her temples, wondering if she should believe her ears.

Ruth said, "I bring him to Minnesota every year for a checkup to keep our health insurance in force. They never even noticed I had a different man. You can borrow him for that, if you like."

Rachel giggled, then let loose with a belly laugh. She ended up crying a few tears, which she wiped away with her sleeve. After turning off the television, they went back into the dining room. She opened a fresh bottle of wine and filled their glasses.

"This had better be our last one, because if you want to go ahead with this, I'll help you," Ruth said. "But, we must get rid of the body tonight. If you think he'd like a burial at sea, we'll have to drive up the coast a ways."

"I'm thinking about it. What do I tell people? Like Archie—the one he goes beachcombing with?"

"Tell him that he's been transferred to a nursing home in Duluth or Reno or somewhere far away."

"How about my daughters and my friends in Minnesota?"

"Initially, you could say he had another stroke and can no longer speak. We can figure out the rest of that later."

"What do I do when I'm done collecting his pension and need a body to bury so I can collect his life insurance? I don't have a handy substitute like you do."

"We'll figure something out."

Rachel gave her a steady look, sighed, and then resolutely nodded her head. "Okay, let's do it."

Nick wasn't wearing his wedding band because his hands had been swelling, and he had no identifying labels on his jogging suit. They worked his feet into a pair of running shoes, which was a job Rachel found emotionally difficult. Then they rolled him into an old blanket and dragged him through the house and breezeway into the garage. He felt like he'd gained fifty pounds when they loaded him, but they managed and shut the door of the camper, going back to the house to wait for it to get a little darker.

"How far do you think we should go?" Rachel asked.

"I don't know. It depends on how well patrolled the beaches are at night. We'll just have to keep driving until we find a likely spot."

"I'd better make a thermos of coffee to take along."

Later, when they drove out of the yard, Ruth spied Vivian skulking up the trail toward her house. "I imagine she was visiting Ben."

"Probably. My house is locked tight, so she can't steal anything unless she breaks a window. Do you think she saw us dragging Nick through the breezeway?"

"I doubt it."

Rachel drove, unconsciously pushing down hard on the gas pedal.

"Sons-a-bitch, lady! You don't want to be stopped

with all the wine we drank, not to mention the, uh, cargo we're carrying."

"I just want to get this done and over with," Rachel said, but she did listen and drove a little more slowly than the posted speed.

Close to Bandon, they found a deserted stretch of beach where they parked. They laboriously tugged Nick along the shore and to the water. They pulled him through the waves, walking until they were up to their hips, and then gave him a push.

He sank from sight.

When they got back to shore, Rachel said the Lord's Prayer, her teeth chattering. They stood briefly, gazing out to sea.

In a hushed tone, Ruth said, "It's only the spirit that counts, I'm certain. Where or how the body goes doesn't much matter." She wrapped her arms around her chest.

"Right," said Rachel with a shiver, wiping tears from her cheeks. "I sure wish we'd have thought to bring some dry pants."

They dashed to the truck and Ruth drove with the heat turned up high. They poured down the coffee and gradually warmed up on the silent ride home.

Chapter 30

AT WORK, VIVIAN'S MIND was not on frying chicken, but she'd performed the task thousands of times, so she worked automatically. Her thoughts twirled in spirals and circles, while she tried to decide on the best way to seduce Ben. All the magazines advised against being too forward, but she had only six weeks before he returned to California. A shock might be the wisest choice. By the time eight o'clock came, she'd planned how to snag the man, and she hurried home to do it.

She showered and sprayed herself with the Shalimar perfume she'd relieved Rachel of. Then she applied only a touch of makeup, since the magazine said heavy foundation enhanced wrinkles. She brushed on mascara, going over her top lashes twice. After she put some gel near the roots of her hair, she bent over and blew it dry. She stood up and whipped it back, feeling a little dizzy. Finally, she stepped into a black thong and pair of black, spike-heeled sandals, whipping on her poplin raincoat.

It was twilight when she sped across the road and down the path that ran alongside the creek, running where she was visible from Rachel's house. When she reached the cottage, she was breathless and her feet hurt, so she stopped and rested for a minute. Composing her face into seductive lines, she climbed up the steps to the porch.

The screen door was locked on the outside with a hook.

"Well, sockcucker!"

She plunked down on the steps, wishing that she'd remembered to check the windows of Rachel's garage, since Ben usually parked his car there. Now she had to walk back home on that rugged trail wearing these shitty heels. She thought about waiting for him to come back home, but it might not be until tomorrow or even next week. There was no way she'd walk the trail in complete darkness and risk breaking an ankle, so she tottered along home.

Past the bridge, she paused to rest behind a tree and saw Ruth and Rachel climb into the truck. It was unusual for them to go places at this late hour. Maybe Nick had taken a turn for the worse and they were going to the hospital. They reached the end of the driveway and turned left, puzzling Vivian even more, because if they were going to the Gold Beach hospital they should have turned right.

She kicked her heels off, stuffed them into her pockets and headed toward her house, walking on the mowed lawn.

Abruptly, she changed her mind. It was the perfect time to pick up some sugar and toilet paper, if Rachel had any extra. And maybe she could dig more deeply into her expensive cosmetics and find some special cream for her eyes.

But all the doors and windows were locked, so Vivian stomped on the creek trail toward home, feeling frustrated and disgusted. Her thong was a little tight and it dug into her ass crack, further irritating her. She paid ten bucks for the thing, but she'd wear it only for seduction, not hiking. She stripped it off, and powered by fury, flung it so hard it snagged onto the branch of a young Sitka spruce that grew on the steep creek bank. She couldn't reach the damn thing from the top of the bank, and the bank was too steep to risk in her heels. Thwarted beyond endurance, she let out a growling scream, which turned to hot tears of helplessness.

It had been one of the suckiest days of her life.

Chapter 31

RACHEL WOKE UP AND stretched, luxuriating in the silky Egyptian cotton sheets on the bed. Through a crack in the draperies, she saw the sun dappling the trees, always a good omen.

And then she remembered.

"Oh, damn."

She sat up and swung her legs to the floor, wondering if maybe the whole thing had just been a dream. The empty space on Nick's side of the bed proved it real. He hadn't even lived in Oregon for a year. She sighed deeply, stood up, and padded to the kitchen to make coffee. She let the coffee drip directly into her cup, then pushed the carafe back onto the burner. After dumping some milk into the poisonously dark brew, she sat at a stool, waiting for the toast to pop up. The coffee tasted too bitter to swallow, so she added more milk and buttered the toast, as if this were an ordinary morning, trying to block out the memory of that ghastly, do-it-yourself burial at sea.

"I can't believe we did that."

She poured a second, less venomous cup of coffee to drink in bed and tried not to look into the family room when she walked by, but she couldn't stop herself. Nick's urine-stained recliner must be discarded, but she needed help getting it onto the truck. Either that or she could drag it to the creek and hope it floated out to sea.

Rachel showered and dressed, then started the sad task of removing Nick's personal cosmetics from the bathroom. After she'd cleaned one shelf, she stopped. *I might need his stuff here since I'm going to be lying about his being dead,* she thought. Trying to make sense of the situation was simply too difficult, so she went outside. Maybe fresh air would relieve her mild hangover and sharpen her mind.

The plants in the greenhouse were beginning to wilt, so she gave them a good soaking. The place seemed to reverberate with memories of Nick. He'd spent considerable time in here, and she enjoyed the pesticide-free produce, so despite the ghost of Nick that surely haunted the place, she finished the job and started back to the house.

Ben was walking by the stream toward the cottage and she hailed him.

"How is Nick doing?" he asked.

"Um, not good. He had a really bad episode last night."

"Is he back in the hospital?"

"Yes, and they transferred him to Medford." That should keep him from trying to visit Nick at the Gold Beach hospital. "He'll most likely be placed in a nursing home in Minnesota after he's stabilized." And that took care of the future.

"I'm so sorry. Is there anything I can do?"

"No. Yes! Will you help me load his recliner onto the truck? It's ruined."

"Certainly. Right now?"

"Yes, if you have time. Do you think you could take it to the landfill for me too?"

"Okay. I was planning to get some groceries today anyway. Do you mind if I drive your truck to the store after I get rid of the chair?"

"Please do." *Whew!*

After he left, she paced around the house aimlessly, feeling hollow and uneasy—-not exactly guilty and not exactly grieving, but a peculiar combination of both.

Without really planning to, she wandered outside and took the trail to Ruth's house.

"I can't believe we did that," Ruth said, opening the back door for Rachel.

Rachel laughed ruefully. "That's exactly what I said when I got up this morning. I haven't dared listen to the news yet. Have any bodies washed up?"

"No. They don't, not always."

"Let's do something to get our minds off of this."

"There's a festival on the beach at Brookings today." Ruth grimaced. "No, forget it. We probably should avoid the ocean for a while."

"Definitely. But we have to get away. What about that abandoned house you told me about? The one that's about eight miles inland."

"That's a good idea. Let's go after lunch. But we'd better take your truck, because my car is too low-slung for that rough driveway."

"Good enough. I just have to wait for Ben to get back from the dump. He hauled the recliner away for me."

• • •

Rachel changed into heavy jeans and ate a tomato and mayonnaise sandwich, forcing herself to swallow it, even though she wasn't hungry. Then she shoved her feet into tall leather boots that she hoped were sturdy enough to protect her from snakebite, should she disturb a rattler when they walked through the tall grass that Ruth said grew around the old house. She grabbed two cans of Pepsi from the refrigerator and sat in the breezeway to wait for Ben.

When he drove in about five minutes later, she motioned him to stop in the driveway. "I'm leaving in a few minutes, so just leave the truck out."

"Okay." He took a bag of groceries out of the cab and handed her the key. "Going to Medford?"

"Medford? Why would I go–oh. No, not until tomorrow. I, um, I just talked to Nick's doctor and the stroke was more severe than they originally thought. They'll know more tomorrow, and I'll drive there then." She'd better make notes to keep track of what was supposed to be going on.

"If you need any help, just let me know."

"Thanks so much. I will." It felt peculiar to pretend that Nick was still alive. Watching Ben walk away, she felt a little like crying, a little like laughing, but mostly she felt confused and numb, finding it difficult to focus.

Thank God for Ruth.

Rachel locked her house and garage, then drove over to pick up Ruth. Her mind was so preoccupied that she turned in to Ruth's driveway too soon and nearly sheared off the mailboxes.

Ruth would have to do the driving today.

Chapter 32

VIVIAN PULLED OUT OF her driveway directly behind Ruth and Rachel, wondering where the two of them were bumming to this time, envious of the gas they could afford to burn. They continued driving south in Rachel's honking big truck; Vivian turned to go to work. What had *they* done to trap husbands with good jobs and big pensions? Perturbed by the unfairness of life, she trudged into the café.

• • •

She worked an extra hour, but it was still light when she got home. Naturally, Dusty wasn't there, but he *had* been. He'd made sandwiches and left the peanut butter and bread on the counter. She sighed, feeling lonely and wondering what the odds were that Ben was home. But it really was too late to visit him or even call anyone. What would she do next year, when she was also a hell of a lot poorer? And even worse, older.

She took a long shower, dried her hair and went to bed. Tomorrow was her day off and she planned to spend it making one last attempt to get close to Ben, clinging like a lichen to his porch steps all day if need be. If there were no results, she'd give up on him and try someone else.

• • •

She caught Ben when he was driving out and flagged him down. "Would you happen to be going into Crusty Beach? I need some transmission fluid. The warning light's on and I don't dare drive it."

"I was just going to the post office, but it's no trouble stopping at the garage. Hop in."

His hair was getting long, which made the few gray hairs attractively visible against the pecan brown.

"Thanks. Dusty will pour it in when he gets home from work, but he hasn't got the time to pick it up." She'd have to put it on her card, but she planned to return it, so there'd be no charge. If the guys at the garage got nasty, she'd pretend that her son had already picked some up, unknown to her.

"You're fortunate to have someone who knows how to do that. I have to pay a garage mechanic to do almost everything except add oil. I don't know much about cars."

"That's about all I know how to do too," Vivian said. "How's the cookbook coming along?"

"It's difficult. I'm trying to write little anecdotes to go along with each recipe, but they seem flat."

"I just keep collecting recipes."

She sat in his spotless car while he went into the post office and then she ran in to pick up the transmission fluid. On the way home, she said, “Would you like to have lunch with me? I’ve got some shrimp salad in the refrigerator, and its terrible good.” She smiled hopefully.

“Thank you, but I’ve already made plans. Maybe some other time.”

“Sure. Thanks for the ride.” *He probably plans on opening a can of soup.* She dumped the jugs by the steps, went into the house, and flopped down on the couch. Tears of frustration and self-pity rolled down her cheeks. She might as well be dead. Then people could visit her tombstone with flowers and feel ashamed about how badly they’d treated her.

Ben would be one of them. He’d read her name and the dates of her birth and death, knowing he’d never done anything to make her life rewarding, not even in a small way. He’d feel guilty and maybe even cry.

Thoughts of tombstones with dates of birth and death gave Vivian an idea. She stopped slobbering, wiped her face on a dish towel, and drove to the nearest cemetery, where she checked out the dates on all of the costliest stones. Three reasonably young women had been buried here recently. After scribbling down their names, she went to two more cemeteries and found more names. Then she went home and dug out the phone book, looking up possible addresses to match the names.

She’d finally discovered a way to meet men. Those poor widowers must be dreadfully lonely and desperate for female companionship.

She was more than willing to come to their aid.

Now, she merely had to figure out a way to approach them.

Chapter 33

RUTH PROPPED OPEN THE carriage doors to the garage and switched on all the lights in the building. It was still dim except for Har's work area in the back. She changed the bulbs from 40 to 75 watts, which helped some. But the interior had never been painted, and the dark, untreated wood absorbed the light. Still, she was able to examine the filthy library table and rocker that she and Rachel had *rescued* from the abandoned house. She hoped that refinishing the furniture might distract Rachel from Nick's death until some time passed, since Rachel, like she, did their grieving internally, hiding all signs of it from the world.

She went into the kitchen, filled a pail with lukewarm water and pine cleaner and grabbed a handful of rags. After she washed the furniture, she was able to tell that it was oak that had suffered some tough use. She stepped outside, dumped out the dirty water, and waited for Rachel, who was walking up her driveway, carrying two books and smiling. She'd changed into cut-off jeans and sandals.

"They were packed away in the guest room," she said, holding up the antique-furniture reference books. "It took me so long to find them, I thought I'd given them to the girls." She handed one to Ruth.

Ruth found a picture of her rocker almost immediately.

"Look! It'll be worth about four hundred bucks after its refinished. It was made around 1900."

Rachel said, "Really! I can't find my table, but similar ones are valued at around that much too. Probably more. These books are several years old."

"Look at this!" Ruth said. "Doesn't it look like the wardrobe that was in the house? And it's valued at over two thousand bucks!"

"We *have* to get the rest of that stuff. We can keep what we want and sell the rest."

Ruth said, "Maybe we'd better see how much we like refinishing first. I know you've done it, but I haven't."

"I can do it if you hate it. I worry about the repair work, though. Nick always did that." A flash of sadness passed over her face. "Do you think Har will help?"

"He *might*." Ruth thought for a minute. "But we should be able to handle the easier stuff ourselves."

"Let's go into Crusty and see what strippers and stuff they have. We still have time today. But we'll probably have to drive to Newport or Medford to find everything."

• • •

They found all the gloves, steel wool, and brushes they needed, but not the citrus stripper that cleaned up with plain water, which Rachel swore by. The owner of the business promised to have some in by the end of the week, so they decided to buy it from him and avoid a trip.

On the drive back home Rachel asked, "How did you manage when your husband died? The grief, I mean."

"I painted and papered the entire house in colors I liked and Har hadn't. And I bought a softer mattress, something he refused to consider." After a moment she added, "I spent a lot of time being pissed off at him for dying and leaving me with so many problems."

"I'm glad I'm not the only one who got pissed off. I thought maybe I was losing it."

"No, it's just part of the grieving process."

Ruth parked in front of Rachel's garage, accepting the offer of some vegetables from the greenhouse.

They sat and relaxed in the screened porch, which was furnished with only two wicker chairs and a packing crate table.

"Is there anyone we can approach to get permission to take the rest of that furniture?" Rachel asked. "I'd really hate to get arrested."

"From what my boss told me, there are no heirs and the place has reverted to the state for back taxes. It's been on the market for about a decade, but there're water problems and no one wants it." She stretched her legs out, pointing her toes and twisting her foot until something in her ankle made a popping sound. "That feels good. Anyway, the house is condemned and slated to be burned for training by the local fire department."

"We'd better clean it out soon. When would be the best time, do you think?"

"On a Sunday morning, when people are either in church or sleeping off their hangovers."

Rachel laughed. "That wardrobe and cupboard might be a little too heavy for us to handle. Maybe we could tell Ben that it's your aunt's place and you're cleaning it out before it's burned down."

"Why not *your* aunt?"

"Because I already told him I had no relatives living in the state. Does it really matter whose aunt it is?"

"I guess not. Yes, go ahead and ask him. He's not likely to check it out."

Chapter 34

ALPHONSO PENROD LIVED ON the outskirts of Brookings. His wife had died six months ago, according to the expensively carved stone at the cemetery. Vivian figured he'd be ripe for a woman, so she parked in front of his driveway, tightened the lug nuts, and let the air out of a back tire. She wiped her hands on a pre-moistened towelette, sprayed herself with a little Shalimar, and dabbed on some lipstick. Her hair was still mousey brown, but she had carefully touched up the roots. Her black eyelet blouse went well with her new white jeans, making her look sharp, she thought, but not whorish. In fact, she felt certain that she looked like a lady. If only she'd had better shoes than the beach thongs she wore, she'd look damn classy. She walked up the curved and wooded driveway, standing up straight, with her gut sucked in.

The wooded property prevented her from getting even the slightest view of the house, but the paved driveway hinted at wealth. She heard a motor running and a thin, middle-aged man appeared around the curve. He wore a natty gray shirt and navy-blue trousers and was mowing the grass bordering the side of the road. She stopped and smiled at him.

He shut the lawnmower off. “May I help you?”

The house was visible through the trees and surrounded by immaculate grounds. It had large, round columns holding the porch roof up and was at least a hundred feet wide.

“I have a flat tire and the lug nuts are on so tight that I can’t get them off,” she said.

“I’d be glad to give it a try,” he said with a smile. “Or maybe you’d prefer to call a garage.”

She glanced at her watch, pretending to be in a hurry. “Oh, would you try it? A garage won’t get here for ages.” He certainly was pleasant, despite being rich. “Boy, is your house big!”

He laughed. “It’s not mine. I’m the caretaker and my wife is the housekeeper. We live in a small house on the property.”

“Oh.” *Crap.*

“The owner is in the Caribbean for a month on his honeymoon.”

“Oooh.” *Crap, crap*, crap. She mentally crossed the guy off her list, dimly realizing that it wasn’t likely that a rich guy would be interested in her for anything, unless she were a hooker. Not unless he’d made his money from a humble start, like building a fleet of portable toilets.

• • •

She was nearly back to Crusty Beach when she spotted a sign for a garage sale. She parked on the side of the road and dumped out her large canvas tote, stuffing her hoard of change into the side pocket. After propping her comb crosswise, so the purse looked full, she walked up the drive.

There were two other customers looking through the piles of mostly women's clothing on the tables. Nearly all of the clothes were in her size, but they were in boring neutral shades, and she loathed blah colors. She was about to leave when she remembered that a magazine article recommended such tones if one wanted to attract upper-class men.

She pawed through the piles until she found a pair of nearly new beige slacks and maneuvered them into her purse. With a little encouragement, she managed to wedge an off-white blazer in too. She stepped out of her rubber beach thongs and slid her feet into a pair of taupe Italian-leather flats that were so comfortable she felt as if she were barefoot. Then she picked up an identical pair in black, which were slightly scuffed, but cost only two dollars. She grabbed a pale yellow camisole, thinking it would look good with her other bargains, and then paid for the black shoes and camisole with quarters, feeling good about saving so much money. She always did well at garage sales.

Chapter 35

RACHEL FOUND HERSELF MISSING Nick the most around lunchtime. Ever since they'd moved here, they had eaten their largest meal in the dining room around noon, bringing each other up-to-date on their activities.

Nick had become fascinated with the plants he'd grown in his greenhouse. Even the humblest heirloom tomato plant had interested him, and his part of the conversation had usually centered on his horticultural endeavors.

Sometimes Rachel helped him water the plants, but she had no idea whether H. carnosa and M. cavendishii would produce food or flowers. Her part of the noontime conversation had been condensed versions of her quilting projects and *some* of the activities she pursued with Ruth. Now she ate a sandwich in her nook while she answered e-mail. For supper she usually had something from the greenhouse.

The family room haunted her with memories of that last day of Nick's life, but she was fond of the spacious room, because it contained the fireplace and opened into the sunny screened-in porch. She moved the furniture around, which helped, but only some. She analyzed her uneasiness about the room and realized that it came more from the cold, white walls than from the fact that Nick had died there. On sunny days the walls shot back too much light for comfort, and on cloudy days they turned gray and lifeless.

After consulting her check balance, she hired a painter to do that room, selecting a light, creamy ivory for the ceiling. She chose the very darkest ivory for the walls, which went well with the camel-colored ceramic tiles that covered the floor. The rounded archway that set the room apart from the foyer kept the paint in the adjoining areas from looking too shabby, but she promised herself that she'd do them soon.

The paint was barely dry when she ordered two area rugs in a lush floral design containing plenty of burgundy, camel and rose. She covered the toss pillows with remnants of rich-looking tapestry, adding heavy burgundy fringes to further unite the scheme. By the time she was finished, the room expressed her taste. It felt more feminine than any room she'd decorated since she'd been married.

• • •

"How did you talk your husband into this?" Vivian asked. She'd dropped in to borrow some beige thread to hem a pair of pants.

Rachel handed her a small spool. "He likes it. He doesn't say much about how I decorate. Just keep the thread; I have another spool."

Vivian glanced around. “I thought you said he’d be in a nursing home, but he must of gotten to come home. Is he in the greenhouse?”

She’d forgotten about that. “No. He’s lying down. We’re letting the greenhouse go, since he can’t get around unless he uses a walker.”

“I didn’t know he was that terrible bad.”

“Yes. And, he can’t really speak well either,” she said, anticipating Vivian’s next question.

“But he keeps getting his pension and health insurance?”

“Yes.”

“Lucky you.” She looked so sourly envious that Rachel found it difficult to keep from laughing. She left soon afterward.

• • •

Ruth and Rachel went twice more to the deserted house and removed all the smaller items. They replaced the weak padlock from the chain barricading the driveway with a heavier one. It seemed *almost* legal when they used their own key to gain entry.

It was time to bring Ben into their unlawful activities.

Rachel walked to his cottage and found him sitting bare-foot on the steps, enjoying the afternoon sun that filtered through the branches. A mop in a pail of dirty water sat on the ground beside him.

“I’d invite you in, but I just mopped the porch.”

“That’s all right. I came to ask a favor. Ruth is

cleaning out her aunt's house and we need help with three heavy pieces of furniture. And, I'll need help taking the camper off the truck so we can use it to haul the stuff."

"Sure. When do you want this done?"

"Sunday morning would be good. The house is only a few miles away. After we haul it, can you help me get the camper back on the truck? There's two week's free rent if you do it."

He grinned. "I can't pass that up. I'd like to rent the cottage again next summer, if that's possible."

"Certainly. Has Vivian stopped bothering you?"

"Yes, now that I'm parking my truck at Ruth's. By the way, how is Nick doing?"

She paused, trying to remember what she'd told him, and decided to tell everyone the same story in order to avoid embarrassing questions should any of her acquaintances talk with each other. Also, she'd better call Archie before he showed up on her doorstep, demanding to see Nick. Maybe she'd better keep the curtains in the bedroom shut too. "Um ... he doesn't have to go into a nursing home, but he can't walk very well. His speech is difficult to understand. I just hope he doesn't have another stroke that leaves him a vegetable. It's bad enough as it is."

"I really feel I should visit him."

"Maybe in a couple weeks. He isn't seeing anybody just now." Lying about Nick's condition wasn't all that difficult when it contained *some* of the truth.

Chapter 36

THE FIRST TIME HE'D SPOKEN to her about renting the cottage, Ben Larkin found Rachel interesting. She had the same crisp manner of speaking as Ruth, with whom he'd become acquainted when he visited his aunt at her hobby shop. As an English teacher, he'd always been more fascinated by varying dialects than most people.

He was also more aware of grammar and flinched every time he spoke with Vivian, whose goal in life seemed to be to seduce and capture him. Lately, she had stopped coming around, but only because he hid in his cottage and parked his car at Ruth's house. It was frustrating to live in this peaceful paradise and have to continually be on guard to avoid the wretched woman.

Rachel, whom he *did* enjoy talking with, had not been over since she'd put the new curtains in his cottage, and he hadn't seen her until today. He sighed, puzzling over why he was so often attracted to married women. Maybe because they were safe. Not that it mattered. Despite the problems with Cindy, he was married to her and married he would stay.

It was because of Cindy and the resulting isolation that he'd pursued writing. Since he was alone, he might as well take advantage of the fact by filling the hours with what he'd been educated to do, despite having diverted it to teaching. He'd been taught the craft required to write, but whether or not he possessed the art he would only find out by writing. With what he'd created so far, it seemed doubtful that he would progress beyond scribbling down facts—handy if he were a journalist, but not adequate for the book he had in mind.

The recipes for cakes, cookies, and pies were stacked in front of him. He'd tried them all and found it amazing that his grandmother had been able to make such delicious food using so few ingredients. And inexpensive ones, at that. The one exception was her Lord Baltimore cake, which he hadn't included in his book but had made and served to his classes at school. The Great Depression had plainly taught Grandma the value of herbs and spices, a variety of which were used in each recipe. It was a good time to publish this cookbook, he felt certain. Now that the price of fuel was eating into people's incomes, recipes for inexpensive meals and desserts would be in demand.

Ben stood up and stretched. He was overdue for a break, and Rachel had given him the perfect excuse. He punched in her number.

"How about if I come over right now and we take that camper off?"

"Okay. Do you think we'll need Ruth too?"

"Wouldn't hurt."

He shut off his phone and tied on his running shoes.

Solitude was great for work, but right now he craved the company of people.

Chapter 37

THE NEXT SUNDAY MORNING, Ruth and Rachel, with Ben tucked between them, drove to the deserted house. Ruth hopped out and unlocked the gate, stepping to the side of the driveway until Rachel drove abreast of her. She relocked the gate and hopped back into the cab.

"Why did you lock that again?" Ben asked as they lurched down the long, overgrown driveway. "We won't be there for that long, I wouldn't think."

"I don't want intruders poking their noses into the place," Ruth said. "They might injure themselves and I'd be stuck with a lawsuit."

They arrived at the house and Ben examined the weathered, boarded-up building surrounded by weeds and brush.

"Didn't you say you're selling it?" he asked.

"No. The state has claimed it for back taxes, but I want Aunt, ah..." Her mind became distressingly blank. She glanced around desperately, her gaze settling on the dash. "Aunt Chevy's furniture."

Rachel made a heroic effort to suppress her laughter, masking it with a hacking cough, but Ben didn't appear to notice.

They entered the dusty house and he quickly explored the interior. "I wouldn't mind living here. It's actually quite sturdy. Paint and shingles and a good cleaning would take care of most of it."

"There's always been a major water problem, even though they drilled two wells. There was a cistern, too, but they still had to haul water almost every summer. And rumor has it that the place is haunted by a couple of boozers who died in the, ah, pantry." She wiped some dust from her hands onto the rear of her jeans, her face getting red.

Rachel said, "I just *love* to hear stories about these old places." She grinned wickedly at Ruth.

"Indeed." Ruth scowled at her. "Let's get busy. I don't want to spend any more time in here than I have to. Allergies."

"Not to mention drunken ghosts lurking around," Rachel said.

After loading the heavy wardrobe onto the truck, they sat down to rest on the rickety steps. Two boys in their early teens drove bicycles up to them and dismounted, clutching the handlebars.

"My mom said to tell you that you're on private property." He looked about fourteen or so, inflated with the importance of his mission. The shorter one nodded in agreement.

Ruth asked, "Just who do you think owns this place?"

“Mom said a real old lady does.”

“And that’s me. Now get out. You’re trespassing on my property.”

“Oh.” They hastily mounted their bikes. “Sorry.” They sped down the drive so rapidly their legs were a blur.

They all laughed as the boys raced around the curve and then quickly loaded the bookcase and breakfront.

Rachel opened a can of Dr Pepper and poured some onto the driveway, making mud. She smeared it onto both license plates, then hopped into the truck.

Ben watched her, keeping his mouth shut. They went about a mile and pulled to the side of the road. Rachel grabbed a rag from under the seat, wiped off the plates and got back into the truck and drove off.

“Do you two mind telling me just what crimes I’ve committed besides illegal trespassing?” he asked.

“You didn’t do anything. You’re just a hitchhiker we picked up.” Ruth smiled and twisted a can of pop off the plastic ring for him.

Rachel guzzled the rest of hers down and crumpled the can. “The state owns the place and is going to torch it soon. It might be a *little* bit of a crime to take the furniture, but it’s *hugely* criminal to burn up antique furniture.”

Ruth said, “And there never was an Aunt Chevy.” She opened a can of pop for herself. “Or any drunken ghosts.”

“Oh, I see. Then this is just a misdemeanor.”

Ruth said, “Ah, not *really*. That wardrobe is walnut, and when it’s all refinished, we should be able to get about three thousand for it.”

"A felony! Oh, brother!" Then he laughed. "But who would even suspect you two of doing something like this?" He chuckled again.

"Exactly," Ruth said.

"Minnesota women," Rachel said with a grin.

"Have you two ever done anything like this before?" he asked.

"Um, not exactly," Rachel said. "We did a small amount of property enhancement this past winter, but that's all." She pulled to the shoulder and let several vehicles pass that were lined up behind her.

Ben frowned, puzzled. "Property enhancement?"

"We cut down a few trees on the property downhill from us," Ruth said. "We wanted ocean views."

"I believe that land belongs to one of the wealthier families on the coast," Ben said, his tone amused.

"Well, then they can afford to donate a little firewood," Rachel said. "And I won't feel bad about getting a little more this winter. The owner never comes around then."

Ben shook his head in disbelief. He said, "What do you say about pruning out a little better view for the cottage? I could come up during Christmas vacation and do some logging with you."

They all laughed.

Ben rubbed the condensation from the pop can onto his jeans. "But I draw the line at kidnapping, murder, and robbing banks."

"Yeah, us too. We pretty much stick with trivial felonies," Rachel said, keeping her eyes on the road and her speed down.

Chapter 38

DRESSED IN HER BLAH-colored pants and blazer, Vivian carried a clipboard when she knocked on the doors of several widows, pretending to be taking a survey. Her major discovery was that men remarry or get girlfriends in a hurry, or at least the half-dozen she'd visited had done so. She must find a way to snap them up more quickly.

But how? She puzzled over it and decided to begin attending the funerals of married women, something she found distasteful, but it was the only way she could beat out the competition. Driving longer distances used up her allowance for gas, so she snagged a couple of twenties from her boss's desk drawer. He'd never miss them.

She almost backed down before she went to the first funeral, having a horrible image of a dozen women all dressed in low-cut black dresses, surrounding the bereaved spouse like a pack of famished wolves. And she, a complete stranger, would have to claw and kick her way through the ravening pack, all the while trying to appear fragile and ladylike.

Tired of wearing the pale yellow chemise and not owning any tops suitable for a funeral, Vivian searched the bulletin boards in Crusty Beach, but she found only garage sales advertising items for small children. She dug in Dusty's closet, but his T-shirts, although black, had huge neon designs printed on them. Becoming a little desperate, she filched a navy blue tank top from a clothesline in town. It was a little loose, but at least it wasn't yellow.

On her day off, she planned to attend three services, two of them in Brookings. After the first funeral, coffee and sandwiches were served in the church basement. Vivian nibbled slowly, listening intently to conversations about the forty-year-old woman who'd left a husband and two grown sons. She gleaned little personal information.

A lady wearing a light gray dress sat next to her. She asked, "How did you know Belinda?"

"We were, er, friends when we were growing up. How about you?" Vivian began to sweat.

The woman said, "She was my oldest sister."

Vivian felt perspiration trickle down the sides of her chest.

"Hot flash?" the woman asked quietly.

"Yeah, I guess so. What's your name?" she asked, merely for something to say.

"Bernice. What's yours?"

Vivian searched her mind for a common name. "Mary. Mary Wilson, back then."

"Oh, yes. You must be the Marianne who always put the spiders into my pockets when we lived in Sacramento."

Vivian felt ready to swoon from tension, but she went along with the spider story, waiting for the woman to see through her. “That’s me, I’m sorry to say.” She smiled, feeling sick, and then hazarded a question. “Were you the one who was always trying to tag along with us?”

“That I was. It was nice of you to come all the way up here for the funeral.”

“Er, I was visiting some friends in Gold Beach and I saw the obituary in the paper. Belinda Burgerfort is such a terrible uncommon name that I figured she had to be the one I knew.” Vivian hurriedly finished her dainty sandwich, frantic to escape before this astute woman caught her in a lie.

“Did you know her husband at all?”

“No.”

“I’ll introduce you to him.”

Now that was more like it.

Which she did, but Belinda’s red-eyed husband was half-a-head shorter than she was, and his head was as hairless as a baby’s ass. She felt relieved that he was too miserable to respond to her. She left immediately afterward, rushing to get to the next funeral on time.

• • •

She needn’t have. The church parking lot on the north side of Brookings had only a few cars in it, all older and rustier than hers. Two men were standing by one of them, sharing a drink from a paper-covered bottle. They wore clean but shabby-looking clothes. She eased her car out of the lot and headed to Gold Beach, where the next funeral was scheduled.

• • •

She was delayed by a roadblock. Two small cars had collided, and she had to take a lengthy detour, which made her too late to attend the service. She did, however, make it to the cemetery, arriving early enough to swipe a modest bouquet of reasonably fresh white roses from a nearby footstone. She stood behind the mourners and tried to hear the minister as he murmured the burial rites. When the crowd thinned, she stepped forward and laid the roses near dear Pamela's grave while looking around for the grieving husband.

A tall and muscular woman of about fifty approached, glaring at her with suspicion. "And how did *you* know my husband?" She snarled the words with such vicious force that saliva shot out of her mouth.

Vivian stepped back. From the corner of her eye she saw another procession approach and knew that one must be Pamela's burial.

The woman took another menacing step toward her, swinging her substantial shoulder bag as if it were a sling.

Vivian spun around and ran to her car as fast as her stolen Italian shoes would carry her.

Chapter 39

AS MUCH AS SHE enjoyed the ocean, Rachel avoided the beaches, having no desire to stumble upon Nick's body, which in her imagination was hideously decomposed but still recognizable. And she did have plenty to do.

During the next two rainy days she discarded most of Nick's clothing. Then she got rid of his fishing equipment, hauling it to the parking lot at the grocery store and putting a *FREE* sign on it. She did the same with some of his tools and most of his hobby equipment. His books, along with hers, filled an entire wall of the family room, but she lacked the heart to sort through them yet.

Her final job was to sort through their collection of over three thousand DVDs. There were many she hadn't viewed, so she began to watch them on the quiet evenings. Others, mostly westerns, she disliked, so she set them aside for Ruth and Ben to look through and take what they wanted.

While she watched, she worked on blocks of appliqué for her quilt. The stylized roses in various shades of pink combined well with the warm green leaves and sparkled against the white background she sewed them to. Nick would never have cared for them, because he'd hated floral designs, but it was her bedroom now, and like the family room, she would decorate it as she chose.

Sleeping in the master bedroom didn't bother her, not after she'd dragged their king-size bed into one of the spare bedrooms and replaced it with a double, antique brass bedstead. She added the new box spring and mattress that she'd purchased when she thought her daughters were coming for a visit. The antique bed stood high off the floor, making it easy on her back when she changed the sheets. She planned to paint the bedroom and the other rooms but not until summer was over. Now, she had furniture to refinish.

• • •

Rachel and Ruth sat at the picnic table in Ruth's yard and drank coffee while they waited for the stripper to soften the varnish on the wardrobe.

"When and where does Har have his checkup?" she asked Ruth.

"I was just thinking about that. At the very end of September. We go to Hibbing for it, but I haven't made the appointment. The RV is small with only two bunks, so we'd have to sleep at a motel. Har can have the RV, which he prefers."

"Okay. I'll pay for the motel and we can split everything else." She rubbed her elbow, which had ached since she'd hauled out the boxes of Nick's belongings. "Nick always used a clinic in Virginia, the few times he went. I worry, though, about Har being able to pull it off. He doesn't look much like Nick, though he has similar coloring."

Ruth said, "I worried about that too. But unless Nick knew some of the clinic employees personally, he's nothing more than a number."

"You're sure Har will go along with this?"

"Yes. He's usually so passive that it's disquieting, but that's good for what we need."

Rachel went to the cement approach of the garage and tested the finish on the wardrobe with a putty knife. "It's ready."

They scraped off as much as they could, filling coffee cans with the citrus-scented slop. Then they used stiff brushes to scrub out the cracks. A few areas needed to have stripper applied a second time, and they again sat at the table and waited for it to work.Rachel said, "Why don't you make Har's appointment for early in the week and I'll request one for the middle of it?"

"Sounds good. Make sure you take the most current drugs Nick was taking and ask for a year's prescription, refillable every three months."

"Why on earth should I waste money on refilling his prescriptions?"

"To avert suspicion. Do you have a drug plan?"

"Yes, thank God. At least I won't have to pay so much."

Ruth said, "We must come up with a way to prevent your clinic from using the same arm for blood as they did at mine."

"Why?"

"Needle tracks."

"I never thought of that."

They scraped the remaining stripper off and then scrubbed the wardrobe with a solution of washing soda and water. Lastly, they rinsed it with the hose.

Rachel checked her watch, which she'd placed on the picnic table. "We have enough time to strip that painted parlor table, too."

"How do we handle it? It's certain to be covered with lead-based paint."

"We'll scrape off as much as possible and then haul it as far as your hose will go to rinse it," Rachel said.

With a twinkle in her eye, Ruth said, "Vivian's at work. We could haul it over there and rinse it at her house."

They just might have done so, but Dusty came home with a friend and the boys spent the afternoon outside working on his car.

Chapter 40

BEN FELT LIKE A total failure. He'd tried all the recipes and put them in order, ready to be inserted into the cookbook, but he couldn't come up with a way to *humanize* them. He didn't want to write a tearjerker about dear old Grandma and her tough life, versions of which had been written by the truckloads and doubtlessly rejected by editors in equal amounts. Disgusted with his apparent lack of talent, he walked over to Ruth's to get his truck to take a drive down the coast. Maybe a break would give him inspiration.

He found Rachel and Ruth outside cleaning up from stripping some of their salvaged furniture. After studying the wardrobe, he asked, "How much is this supposed to be worth?"

"Look it up in those books on the table," Ruth said. She was filling a pail with soap and water from the hose. She dumped in some brushes and putty knives and swirled them around.

Ben sat down and began to page through one of the books until he found the section containing wardrobes.

They all looked the same until he studied them closely. He soon found one that was identical. The value surprised him.

"Will you really be able to get this much for it when it's refinished?"

Rachel said, "Yes, if we can find a buyer."

He looked through the book, his interest becoming avid when he found a dresser and a side table that matched the ones his grandmother had given him.

"Planning to sell some old furniture for a little extra cash?" Ruth asked.

He smiled. "No. I found a dresser identical to the one my grandmother gave me. I think I can tie the furniture and the recipes together with some anecdotes."

"That ought to be interesting," Rachel said. She stood by him and he pointed out the furniture. "Except, depending on their ages, I think your grandparents might have been wee infants when this stuff was manufactured."

Ben did some rapid calculations. "You're right. Maybe it came from my great-grandparents. I have to do a little research. But the idea feels right."

"Let us know what you find out."

He nodded. His grandma's youngest sister, Sylvia, was still alive, and he decided to give her a call and ask her if she knew anything about it.

He asked, "Whose books are these?"

"Mine," Rachel said.

"May I borrow this one for the evening?"

"Sure. Take both of them for as long as you want."

He did, cradling them in his arm. He also changed his mind about taking that drive. If he could tie

Grandma's furniture into the cookbook, he could bring it to life. He had a strong hunch that the book would sell. He sped home on the creek trail, filled with anticipation and eager to talk with his great aunt. He was worried that she might die before he could find out the stories behind the furniture, though he planned to make the stories more interesting if need be. He dumped the books onto the table and dug out his address book, smiling as he punched in Sylvia's number.

Finally, he'd hit on the perfect idea for his book.

Chapter 41

WITH INCESSANTLY ROTTEN LUCK in her search for men in the outside world, Vivian decided to bring them to her home by having a rummage sale featuring men's items. She'd hold it outside, in front of the trailer. In a feverish orgy of preparation, she slapped a coat of turquoise paint on the steps and door and used the rest of the paint she'd purchased to cover the paneling in her living room. Too lazy to clean the brush, she left it in the nearly empty can and stomped the lid shut with her foot, then flung the whole works into the trash.

Now, to acquire some masculine items to sell.

Her first thought was to lift stuff from Rachel and Ruth's garages, but she quickly dismissed the idea. Rachel currently kept the place locked up even when she was at home. And Ruth's husband had very few tools, except for the ones he used to carve with. It would be just her luck to have Har come over and lay claim to the tools, and maybe even contact the sheriff.

She would simply have to scratch together stuff from somewhere else.

But where? One thing she would not do was shoplift from stores. She did have *some* standards. Then too, most of the stores had video cameras, making it easy to identify thieves.

On her break at work, she took off her hairnet and combed her hair. She sat with Jill and chatted, as usual.

"Where did you get that windbreaker?" she asked Jill. "It looks expensive."

"It flew out of the back of a truck that pulled out of the parking lot at the beach on Airing Point. I waved at the people, but they never looked back, so I kept it."

"Their loss is your gain. I wisht I could get that lucky."

"Crumbs, most of those tourists leave things lying in the open. I saw a Nikon camera in a truck cab and the door was open. Anyone could take it. Must be nice to have money."

"That's for sure." *Eureka!* It would be even safer if she *collected* merchandise from people who lived out of state.

During her next two days off, Vivian dressed as a tourist and haunted public access roads and pull-offs near the ocean. She chose to pick up bargains from people with new vehicles because she figured they could probably afford the loss. She managed to find quite a few tools, even a huge set in a metal box that she could barely lift into her car. Unfortunately, the owner's name had been etched onto the box; she'd have to sell each tool separately.

To round out the tools, she went to a few garage sales, carrying her empty canvas purse and filling it with crap she figured men would buy. Whenever she found a box of free items, she grabbed them up, knowing she could sell most of the things for a quarter if she cleaned them up. She treated herself to a couple of DVDs and some almost new jeans for Dusty. Because of his job, he hadn't stayed with his father for several weeks in a row as he'd done before, but only visited during a couple of weekends. Whatever the reason, his father no longer bought him the costly wardrobe he formerly had. She'd have to buy him some clothes, even though he was becoming particular about what he'd wear. So be it; if he didn't like what she bought for him, he could buy his own.

She sat at her table and wrote ads for her yard sale and hoped for dry weather.

Chapter 42

THE SUMMER TURNED OUT to be warmer than usual, and Ruth thought it more pleasant than any other since moving here. She credited much of that to becoming friends with Rachel. After the two of them had finished stripping the furniture, they glued the loose joints, sanded the pieces, then stained them. They brushed on a generous coat of polyurethane, and after a light sanding, applied a mixture of poly and mineral spirits, adding layer upon layer with a rag, until the wood glowed. The furniture looked so beautiful that they split most of it between them, selling only the wardrobe and the enormous breakfront. Rachel kept the library table for her family room and put two parlor tables into the cottage to replace the cable rolls. Ruth kept the rocker and bookcase.

After they helped the buyer load his furniture, Ruth pocketed her share of the money, planning to use it to pay for the trip to Minnesota, figuring that most of the cash would go into the gas tank.

Rachel stuffed hers into her vest pocket. "This should pay for having the cottage wiring upgraded. It was done in the twenties and is actually dangerous. By the way, do you want some dangerously ripe tomatoes?"

"Sure." They walked toward the greenhouse. "My house was built around the same time, but it was rewired in the late sixties, so it *should* be fine," Ruth said.

Rachel pulled the key from her jeans and unlocked the door. They picked the red tomatoes, placing them into plastic grocery sacks that were kept in there for that purpose. They did this regularly, trying to keep up with the produce as it ripened.

"I think we have them all," Rachel said, looking around. "No, there's still that plant in the corner to pick."

"Are you going to continue gardening?"

"I think so, but I'm not planting this much next season. I've had to toss so much out. And I'm *never* going to can again."

Ruth bent down to grab a tomato that had rolled under the table. She added it to the sack and pushed her hair behind her ears. "Not even to make a few jars of bread and butter pickles?"

"Well, maybe them. They're so good. And some peach jam, which I love."

"Just call when you're ready and I'll help."

• • •

And so the summer spun quickly by, as did most of them. Ben left at the end of August, leaving Ruth with a peculiar kind of loneliness; the man had been helpful and interesting, despite being extraordinarily private. Ruth realized that she knew very little about the man, but she did like him.

• • •

It poured buckets of rain at the beginning of September, greening up her parched lawn. It cut the fire danger, always a lurking thought of horror with the resinous evergreens growing so lushly in the region. The rain stopped abruptly and the warm September weather made it difficult to stay indoors. Ruth spent all available time forking compost into her flower gardens.

The sudden volume of water also brought the large gopher snakes out of the creek gulch where they'd lived peacefully all summer. Ruth discovered this when she was pushing a load of compost to her azalea bushes and heard a scream of terror coming from Rachel. She dashed to the bridge, crossing at a gallop, yelling for her friend.

"I'm in front of the garage. Don't come close! There's a huge snake in front of the garage door and I think it might be a rattler."

Ruth peered cautiously around the building at the eight-foot-long snake. "It's not venomous; it's a gopher snake." She laughed at Rachel, who stood, pale and shivering, on top of her camper.

"Well, shoot the damned thing. There's a gun in my bedroom closet and it's loaded. I'm not coming down till that thing's dead!"

Ruth hadn't realized that Rachel was so terrified of

snakes. Instead of making a mess, she grabbed a handful of pebbles and flung them at the creature, chasing it away. She helped Rachel down from the truck. "The creek is so full that they're seeking high ground. Don't worry, they're harmless."

"Harmless! That one damned near gave me a heart attack!"

"It *is* the biggest one I've ever seen, but usually they stay in the brush. Sometimes they climb into trees for eggs and birds. And there's another variety around here that'll climb into the shrubs and small trees if you chase it."

Rachel shuddered. "Chase a snake? No chance in hell!" Her eyes darted nervously around the yard. "Aren't there supposed to be rattlesnakes in Oregon?"

"I guess, but mostly in the high desert-like region. At least that's what I was told."

They went into the house to discuss their upcoming trip to Minnesota.

Rachel said, "I'm not telling my daughters that I'll be in Minnesota. Too many complications. I just hope I don't run into them by accident."

"I thought you might want to see them, even for a few hours."

"No. I'll tell them about Nick when they threaten to come for a visit. And you can bet they'll come with their hands open, expecting that their father left them the entire estate in his will."

Ruth was shocked at what Rachel had said. "Are they really that greedy?" she asked gently.

Rachel looked sad. "Yes, I'm sorry to say. So

many in that generation feel entitled to things without sweating for them. Maybe they'll outgrow it."

"Makes me glad I never had kids."

Chapter 43

THE TRIP TO MINNESOTA went without a hitch, as did Har's physical when he stood in for Ruth's husband. When he went for the examination impersonating Nick Christenson, however, things became a little hairy. All three were in the camper at the parking lot of Rachel's clinic, trying to convince Har to wear an elastic bandage on the arm from which his blood sample had been drawn. He resisted, so standing a little behind him, Ruth said, "You have a tender bruise right here." She gave his funny bone a rap with a screwdriver handle.

He grabbed his elbow, cradling it in his hand.

"If I wrap it, you won't bump it hard enough to hurt and it'll heal faster."

Har willingly submitted, and Ruth wound the bandage around his arm, looking guilty.

Rachel rubbed her shoulder. "A woman's got to do what a woman's got to do."

Ruth looked straight ahead, then turned to Rachel, nodding her head with a shadow of a smile.

Later, while they sat in the clinic waiting room, an acquaintance of Rachel's plunked down next to her.

"Hey, long time, no see!" she chirped, with a big toothy grin.

Not her! "Lucy. Um, how are you?" Rachel asked, smiling weakly. She fought panic while listening to Lucy's inane chatter. She struggled to plan her next move while the woman gabbed on. She became tenser by the minute, feeling a strong desire to scream and run away. Instead, she smiled and nodded, which seemed enough feedback for the garrulous woman. Lucy had known Nick only slightly, so if she were lucky, perhaps she wouldn't realize that Har, who was sitting next to her, was not her husband.

Ruth, on the other side of Har, sat as rigidly as if she were wearing a steel corset. She also listened to the woman yammer away about nothing of consequence. She caught Rachel's eye and nodded almost imperceptibly, then casually picked up an oncology pamphlet from the table in front of them.

Rachel nodded back.

Har sat tranquilly, gazing down at his loosely crossed legs, decidedly oblivious to the nerve-wracking situation, and indeed, to almost everything except his bandage, under whichhe tucked his finger every now and then.

"I heard that you moved to Oregon, but it must've been nothing but gossip." Lucy stopped and looked at her, clearly waiting for confirmation.

"Har—ah, my husband's just here for a yearly checkup today." Her answer seemed to satisfy Lucy, but Ruth smirked at her ambiguity.

"You'll have to stop in and visit one of these days. Or are you still working?"

"Yes, I'm working, but I have a different job."

Lucy asked, "What are you doing now?"

The woman didn't care, Rachel knew, but she loved to glean information to add to her continual gossipy conversations. "I'm refinishing antique furniture. I work on it with another woman."

"Where's that? I have an old rolltop desk that needs to be redone." She leaned toward Rachel, waiting for an answer.

"West of Hibbing."

Ruth chortled loudly, pretending that she'd read something highly amusing from the oncology pamphlet.

Nick's name was called and Rachel escaped into the examining room, accompanied by Ruth and Har. As soon as he had his blood pressure taken, Ruth left. Rachel became increasingly tense, worrying about going to prison for insurance fraud. Har sat quietly, looking at his legs.

The doctor came in. He updated Nick's chart, wrote a prescription for a year's worth of blood pressure pills and gave the same basic advice that he'd given them before. He pretended to *know* Har, jovially asking him a few questions about fishing, which Har naturally didn't answer. He told Rachel to bring him back for another examination in a year, if he didn't have to see him sooner, and that was that.

• • •

They were traveling back through Montana when

Rachel said, "You were right. We *are* nothing more than numbers. I think I could have brought an Australian Aborigine into that room and the doctor wouldn't have thought anything of it. He probably would just ask him if he'd done any fishing lately."

Ruth pulled to the shoulder to let a bus pass her. She said, "Yes, I know. People over forty are often invisible to others, especially younger people. You have your daughters, though, so at least you'll always have them."

"They aren't very interested in what I'm doing. They generally call to tell me what they've been up to but only what they want me to hear." Rachel sighed. "When we lived close to them, they borrowed money now and then and dropped off their pets when they went on trips. They didn't visit otherwise, and I never felt particularly welcome at either of their places, so I rarely went."

Ruth said, "I wonder if it's just you?"

"Other women have told me the same thing. The only value they see in us is free babysitting services."

"Sure is different from the fairytale life you see in the movies, isn't it?"

"Yes. If I had it to do again, I'd think long and hard before having any kids."

• • •

After daylight saving time ended, Rachel began the laborious process of painting the house. She started in her bedroom, which she painted the palest pink that was on her appliquéd quilt blocks. Then, tired of the darkness created by the continually closed draperies, she bought more sheer curtain panels, hanging them behind the drapes. After dark, she went outside to check if she'd need still more for privacy and found that light showed through, but nothing else was identifiable.

She wanted a lushly upholstered chair and a side table to place in the window bay, but she decided to wait for sales. Maybe she could buy a used chair and make a slipcover. There was no hurry; the old wooden chair currently sitting there would serve for the time being.

She did buy an extra television with a large screen, spending many luxurious evenings in bed eating potato chips while she watched *Gone With the Wind* and other favorite movies in their entirety, with no snide comments from a spouse who'd prefer to watch a western. She missed Nick, but being a widow did have its advantages.

She saw Ruth a couple times a week and got e-mail from a few friends, including Ben, who wrote quite often. For now, it was enough, although she knew that she'd want to make more friends eventually.

But she wouldn't until she buried the phantom husband who still occupied one of the spare bedrooms.

Chapter 44

BEN CALLED RACHEL TO reserve the cottage for two nights during Thanksgiving weekend. "It's usually quite warm, and there was still enough wood under the porch to heat it using the Franklin stove. I know you worry about the wiring when I use that electric heater."

"I do. In fact, I'm having the cottage rewired in the spring before you come for the summer. Unless you'd like to do it in lieu of rent."

He laughed. "No, thanks. I can put a new cord on a lamp, but that's about my limit. Actually, I wanted to walk around with you and mark the trees we'll cut during Christmas vacation."

"Good idea. Bring rainwear, though. We get quite a bit more than you do, I think."

Ben looked out his kitchen window in northern California. It wasn't raining, but the day was cool and heavily overcast. "You're right," he said. They chatted for a few minutes and then he hung up, feeling cheered.

He went back to reading the themes he's assigned his senior class to do, grading them while he did so.

Most were adequate, and a few were dreadful, written by individuals whose talent definitely lay in other directions. Two or three were quite good, but no more than that. Ever since he'd begun to teach, he'd hoped to find a gifted student whose writing was exceptional and filled with possibilities, but it hadn't happened. He finished checking papers and fought off the increasing disillusionment he'd found in his career. He had only continued to teach because he wished to live here, close to his wife, Cindy.

He had married her before he knew that she came from a moneyed family, something she'd kept secret so she could be certain he married her for love. Even after she had confessed, they had never used a penny of her trust fund, but they did keep the health and life insurance policies she'd had since her birth. They lived happily on what he made. Then she'd developed an inoperable brain tumor. Because the trust fund stipulated that unless she had children the fund would stop with her death, she had dipped into the horded money and bought a manor on ten acres, putting it into Ben's name only. She'd transferred all the money she could into accounts accessible to him, knowing that her medical bills would be paid in full from the health insurance policy that was a part of her trust. As long as she lived, the money would continue to be deposited into her and Ben's joint savings account.

Now Cindy lay in a coma in a private nursing home. Because of the wonderful care she'd been given, she looked much the same as she had five years ago. Her hair was still blonde and shiny, her skin ivory and flawless. They even applied a bit of cologne after they exercised her limbs and bathed her. Although she looked the same, she never spoke or opened her eyes. She was able to swallow, so they fed her by mouth. The tumor grew and Cindy still lived, breathing in and out, with no other indications that she was still alive, except for an occasional heartbreaking sound somewhere between a chuckle and a whimper.

The love Ben felt for her had not died, but it had gradually turned into a tender pity. He would never abandon her, not after all she'd done to insure his future. Sometimes, and only for her sake, he wished she would stop breathing.

Chapter 45

VIVIAN WOKE UP AT the beginning of November with the awareness that she despised Jerry, the charter boat owner she'd met at her yard sale. In her frantic hurry to catch a man, not wealthy, not gorgeous, but *employed,* Jerry had seemed adequate, even attractive. He was an expert bed partner, something she'd done without for longer than she cared to admit.

In her infatuated state, there was much she was willing to overlook, such as four children in grade school over whom he had full custody. And his large house, beautifully finished on the outside, but with sheets tacked up on the interior stud walls for privacy. It was temporary, he had told her. She'd finally woken up from her hazy state of mind, however, to notice that the sheets were positively grubby. Clearly, temporary had already been a long time.

Still, she was willing to give him the benefit of the doubt. Taking care of kids and working full-time were exhausting, and he probably hadn't had the energy to finish the house. After spending a Sunday night at his rural home, she waited until he went to work and the kids left for school, and then took a walk, visiting his closest neighbor, who lived a few acres away.

She walked up the driveway to find an older couple sitting outside of a manufactured home, soaking up the weak mid-autumn sunshine.

"Hi! I'm Vivian Snell and I'm visiting Jerry. I was out walking and wondered where you got your cute mailbox at."

The man stood up from a folding lawn chair and extended his hand. "I bought it in Fargo before we left. I'm Larry Nelson and this is my wife, Emma." He opened another lawn chair for Vivian.

"Have you lived here long?" she asked.

"Moved here from North Dakota about ten years ago. We had a beet farm—near a thousand acres. Wanted to retire somewhere without snow or tornadoes."

She listened to the man tell the story of his life, while his wife sat still, seemingly in a stupor. During a lull in his monologue, Vivian jumped in and said, "Yeah, I'm from central California and it was too hot there during the summer. I like it better here—nicer people and less crime. Do you know Jerry at all?"

Emma finally opened her mouth. "A little. He spends a lot of time at work and then his live-in housekeepers care for the kids. He's busy."

"Yes, he is." How many *housekeepers* had he had? *Did the old woman actually believe that?*

"He goes through them pretty fast. There's a new one about every six months." She scratched her armpit vigorously, and then continued, "I hope you last longer, but the place is hard to keep clean. Too bad he can't finish it."

"Can't or won't?"

"Can't. Something about an archaic zoning law for that bit of land. He's allowed to live there, but he can never finish the house or sell it. He's had a lawyer working on it for five years."

So that's where most of his money went, why he never had enough to take her out to supper, and why he drove that smelly old truck. The farmer rattled on and Vivian nodded at the appropriate moments, but when he went into the house to use the bathroom, she made her escape. She promised to visit the old lady again, although she knew that she wouldn't.

Now that she knew about Jerry, she'd ease him out of her life so she could find someone closer to her needs. Someone with fewer problems and more money, or at least a better job. And she had to hurry. In seven months Dusty would graduate and leave, his support payments would cease, and she'd be nearly destitute.

Chapter 46

RUTH WAS BACK TO working two days and three days a week at the store, which was usual for the rainy months. At home, she spent many hours hooking rugs. Even so, she had plenty of time to search through the forest below her house with Ben and Rachel, marking the trees they planned to cut. While they did so, it drizzled lightly, enough to get their shoes soaking wet. They plodded through the woods, slowly becoming chilled, but they finished the job.

“I have my coffee pot all set up,” said Ben, when they neared the cottage.

“You don’t have to ask me twice,” said Ruth, shivering.

They stepped into the porch and took off their soggy shoes, which Ben picked up and placed on the Franklin stove. The cottage was pleasantly warm, and Ben piled two more chunks of wood on the grate before dumping water into the reservoir of the coffee pot. They all sat down.

Ruth said, “This is the coldest I’ve ever known it to

get around here. It was only forty when I left the house this afternoon."

Rachel asked Ben, "Was it warm enough in here this morning?"

"It was nippy when I crawled out of bed, but the stove heated it quickly enough."

"Next year I'll hire someone to put some insulation in the attic," Rachel said. "But the wiring *has* to come first."

Ruth asked, "There's no insulation up there?"

"None. I guess it was intended for summer use only." Rachel turned to Ben. "If it's any colder at Christmas, you'll have to stay in one of my guest rooms."

"And if her kids come up for a visit, I have a spare bedroom upstairs."

Ben got up and poured coffee. "Agreed. What about Nick? He'll be left alone a lot when we're out in the woods. Does he need any help with things?"

Rachel said, "Um, I'll have a health-care person come in on those days. Insurance covers it for three days a week, and that should be enough to get that wood out."

They discussed what they'd need to rent and buy for their logging venture. It turned out that Ben owned an old chainsaw; he'd put himself through college by cutting firewood. As they talked, a thrill of eagerness bubbled up in Ruth. She supposed it was an adrenalin rush at the thought of another illegal adventure. There was only a slight chance that they'd be caught, but the risk added zest to her usually placid life.

• • •

Ruth invited Rachel to her house for Christmas dinner. They ate the meal, served on everyday dishes at the kitchen table. The only holiday touches were candles and a Christmas bouquet.

"This is perfect," said Rachel. "It's just enough to make it special."

Har ate neatly, neither agreeing nor disagreeing. After the meal he went back to the garage.

After piling the dishes onto the counter and putting away the leftovers, they went into the living room and pushed furniture around until they came up with a good arrangement incorporating the refinished bookcase and rocking chair. Then they had mugs of hot apple juice spiked with brandy and cinnamon sticks.

"This is really good," Rachel said, sipping her drink. She pulled her stockinged feet up under her on the plaid couch.

"My mother used to make it for holidays. Har can't drink alcohol anymore, and I rarely have any alone, so this is a treat for me." She refilled their mugs with the rest of the apple juice and added brandy. She took a tiny sip, then blew on it. "I have a hunch that Ben might be a little interested in you."

Rachel whipped her head around to face Ruth. "How so? I've never picked up on anything like that." She stirred her drink with a cinnamon stick.

"It's mostly that he takes little peeks at you when he thinks you aren't looking."

"He *is* married, so it could never go anywhere. And come to think of it, I'm still a married woman, sort of." She laughed ruefully.

Ruth chuckled, then proposed a toast. "To our pension checks. May they never end till we want them to."

• • •

It was warm after Christmas when Ben came for three days. Amazingly, it rained only at night. They logged the property, cleaned up the chips and logging debris, and then disguised the stumps like they had the year before.

They were nearly done but were tired and needed a break. Rachel handed out cans of Dr Pepper, which Ruth guzzled thirstily. She had worked up a sweat from the exercise on the unexpectedly warm day. Again, she observed Ben studying Rachel, knowing that her friend's life could become difficult if she chose to respond. But perhaps Ben was only admiring her. According to Rachel, he hadn't made any moves.

While Ben hauled his luggage to his car, Ruth helped Rachel straighten up the cottage. "Ben was really eyeing you when we were working in the woods. Did you notice?" She bundled up the used sheets and tied the trash bag shut.

"Yes," Rachel said, looking a bit uneasy. She poured some bleach into the toilet and shut the lid. "After you mentioned it, I really watched him. I doubt he'll do anything other than look, though."

Ruth felt worried. "I hope you're right."

Chapter 47

AFTER THEY FINISHED CLEANING the cottage, Ruth went home and Rachel stayed to sweep the steps. Before she finished, Ben walked toward her, coming from the woods.

"Forget something?" she asked.

"My umbrella. I'd hung it on a nail just inside the porch door. It looks like rain, and I want a walk in the woods before I start home."

They parted, Ben heading down the hill and Rachel for home, reaching the mailbox a little ahead of Vivian.

They spotted Har at the same instant. He was lying on the side of the driveway with a carving beside him.

"Oh, God!" Vivian screeched. "He's dead."

Rachel raced over and felt his wrist for a pulse. "No, he's just unconscious. I'll call Ruth." She pulled her phone from her jacket pocket and shakily punched in the number. "I think you'd better come down to the mailbox. Bring a blanket. Har's passed out on the ground here."

"Oh, brother! Should I call an ambulance?"

"No. *Don't do that.* Vivian is here too."

"I'll be right there."

Vivian checked her watch and paced around, plainly wanting to escape. "I'm running a little late for work. Do you mind staying here alone?"

Thank God! "No, that's fine. Ruth will be here in a minute." As Vivian turned away and hurried back to her house, Rachel placed her umbrella over Har's face to keep the rain off, though she knew it didn't matter to the man anymore.

Ruth jogged toward her but slowed down when Rachel shook her head. "He's not breathing, but I told Vivian that he was. She seemed ready to have hysterics. Besides, I didn't know what, um, what you wanted to do with him."

Ruth said, "Sons-a-bitch! I wasn't ready for this." She clutched the blanket to her chest, the drizzle getting them soggier by the minute.

"What *do* you want to do?"

She stared at him for a long time. "Looks like it's time for another burial at sea."

"Ew. Okay. But Vivian is looking out her window, so we'd better attend to Har as if he were alive."

"Good Lord, yes!" She flung the blanket onto his body and they propped his head onto the carved log, arranging his hands on his chest. He had wet his pants but not soiled them.

After a few minutes, Vivian left her house and drove out, pulling over onto the end of Ruth's driveway. "Is he doing okay?"

"He's coming out of it, but he's still a little groggy," Ruth told her.

"What a relief." She drove off.

Ruth said, "It's a good thing we have the four-wheeler for another day." She ran to the garage and drove it out.

They tried to load Har onto the trailer, struggling mightily, but the big man weighed more than they could handle.

"Now what should we do?" Rachel asked. "I hope to hell no cars come along." She kept darting looks up and down the road, praying that no one would drive by. The rain began to pour down harder.

Finally, they spread the blanket on the ground and rolled Har onto it. They poked a hole into the blanket with the hook from the winch and dragged him into the garage. Ruth ran back for the Virgin statue, and Rachel emptied both of their mailboxes. Thoroughly wet and icy cold, they stumbled into Ruth's cozy warm house.

They toweled dry in Ruth's bedroom and dressed in heavy caftans she pulled from her closet. They had just thrown their clothes into the dryer when someone pounded on the front door. For some reason, Rachel expected the cops and her heart began to thud heavily.

It was Ben. "I thought I might find you here. I'm leaving. I'll let you know if I can make it for Easter."

Rachel said, "That's fine. I'm not renting to anyone else."

After he left, Ruth let out a quavering sigh. "Do you suppose he could tell we dragged something on the road?"

"I don't think so. It's pouring so hard I think it erased the drag marks." Rachel took a deep breath and asked,

"What are we going to do with him? He's way too heavy to lift into the truck. Please—not dismemberment."

"I'm not cutting him up. And, getting someone to help is out of the question too." She shuddered, rubbed her hands together briskly, and put some water in the kettle for tea. She readied the teapot and placed cups and an unopened bottle of brandy on the table.

Rachel shivered. "Absolutely not. And we're not trying a do-it-yourself cremation on him. We couldn't get the fire hot enough and the smell ... Ugh."

"I don't want to bury him here. Every time I passed his grave, I'd feel horrid, even though he never spoke one word to me in his entire life."

They sipped their brandy-spiked tea and had a second cup before they warmed up. Numerous ideas, increasingly impractical and irreverent, occurred to them as the level of the brandy dropped.

"I think I have a good way. Do you have a life jacket?" Rachel asked, her voice slurring a little.

"Yeah, there are a couple old ones in the garage."

"How about if we wait until it's darker, then put one on him and drag him to the creek with the ATV. With any luck at all, he'll float all the way to the ocean."

Ruth thought for a minute, squinting her eyes nearly shut. "It's about all we can do. The creek's pretty high now. It should work. I'll have to check his pockets and take his rings off." She winced at the thought.

"I'll help you." She stood up and looked out the window at the pouring rain. "This is sooo depressing."

Ruth drained her fourth cup of tea, and said, "Look at the bright side. We still have until September to find someone to impersonate our husbands for their exams. That's months away."

"Lots of time," Rachel agreed cheerily.

"Yup. More tea? Then we'd better attend to the funeral duties while we can still stand."

"Sounds like a plan to me."

Chapter 48

VIVIAN WAS LONELY AND at loose ends after she dumped Jerry, so on the day after Har fainted, she stopped in to see Ruth. "How is your husband? It scared me something terrible to see him lying on the ground like that. I thought for sure he was a goner."

They were in Ruth's aqua kitchen drinking coffee strong enough to melt tires. Ruth slugged down a large mug of the thick beverage, but she still looked tired, as if she'd been awake half the night. Despite that, she was her usual well-mannered, but reserved self.

"So, how is he?" she asked again, glancing around the unusually disordered kitchen.

"He sprained his knee when he fainted, but he's doing well. They kept him overnight to run some tests." She shifted uneasily in her chair. "I'll pick him up this afternoon."

"Glad to hear that." Vivian politely swallowed more coffee, the sides of her tongue quivering at the bitterness of the brew. It reminded her of dandelion milk.

Ruth stood with the coffee pot hovering over Vivian's cup. "More?"

"No!" She grasped the top of her cup, her hand covering the entire thing. "Thanks anyways. I'd better get moving. I can't be late for work."

"Thanks for stopping by."

Vivian left, gripping the magazine she'd nipped off of Ruth's table and hidden under her arm beneath her shirt. As soon as she got into her house, she paged through it quickly and thrust it into the garbage can. The *Smithsonian* had nothing of interest for her between its covers.

• • •

At work that day, she visited the boss's office to grab a little extra cash, only to discover a new desk installed in the room. All the drawers were locked.

She was in dire need of some money to pay her phone bill, which was overdue. Her chance came when there was a lull in customers and Glenda, the cashier, went on her break, leaving Vivian in charge of the till, something she occasionally did.

A party of four paid for their meal with a hundred-dollar bill. Instead of placing it in the register, Vivian dropped it onto the floor, slipped off her loafer, grasped the bill with her bare toes, and shoved it into her shoe. The security camera only filmed what she did above the waist, so she felt certain that she'd get away with it. It might even pass as an error, being an even number. She hoped Glenda didn't get fired, but *she* had a husband to support her.

And Vivian had only herself.

Chapter 49

RUTH KNEW THAT VIVIAN was light-fingered, but *when* had the woman found the time to steal her magazine? It must have been when she stood up to get the coffee pot to refill their cups. She told Rachel about it on the phone. "It would have taken only seconds for me to get it, but I suppose that's enough time."

"I've avoided her ever since you told me about her stealing, but it wasn't soon enough to keep her from taking a full bottle of Shalimar perfume. I smelled it on her when we found Har on the road that day, and I'm sure it's too costly for her to *buy*."

"I suppose she thought you wouldn't recognize it."

"She thought wrong. By the way, what magazine did she take?"

"The *Smithsonian*."

Rachel chuckled. "I have trouble imagining Vivian reading that."

"Me too, but it's gone just the same. At least I was done reading it."

• • •

Ruth was surprised when Vivian stopped by the next morning, and the day after that, also. Both times, she told the woman that her husband was resting in bed. "He tires easily and is supposed to keep weight off that knee. It was a severe sprain."

"It's like he's not here anymore," Vivian whined. "And it's the same with Nick Christenson. You and Rachel both have husbands like ghosts, but you still keep getting big pension checks." Envy poisoned her expression.

"The mines are a dangerous place to work, but people are paid well for taking risks. The pensions are high for the same reason." Ruth wondered why she bothered to explain it. She felt uneasy in the face of Vivian's repeated expressions of envy, which could easily turn the woman into an enemy. "I'll let you know when he's up and around."

Vivian nodded but said nothing, and the silence stretched on until the phone rang. Although it was only her boss asking her to work an extra day, she spoke to her like she was a long-lost friend, grateful that the diversion allowed her to escape from an uncomfortable conversation.

• • •

Within a week, a body washed up on shore a little south of Gold Beach. Ruth and Rachel spent a tense afternoon at Rachel's house, waiting for the news. Finally, it came over the radio that the body was that of a female.

Rachel slumped over in relief. “I wonder how long it’ll be before we don’t have to worry about the guys being found anymore.”

“I’m sure you don’t have to. I suppose it’ll be a couple more weeks for me, depending on the temperature and currents and stuff.”

“Oh, yuk! And I was just beginning to enjoy eating meat again.” She said it with a rueful grin.

Ruth laughed. “Yes, me too. By the way, Vivian has made some jealous squawks about us having invisible husbands and big pension checks.”

“Damn it anyway! We put in our time to get what we have. But I doubt she sees it that way.”

“As long as she keeps her distance, we’re okay. But she’s been over three times since Har’s, uh, accident. I’ve always said he’s in bed.”

Rachel wrinkled her brow. “Oddly enough, she’d been over to my house three times this past week too. I told her that Nick was in bed too.”

“Oh, Lordy!” Ruth said. “We’re going to have to think of something different or she’s going to get suspicious, if she isn’t already. Maybe we can buy one of those inflatable male dolls from a Web site. One of those sex toys.”

When Rachel stopped laughing, she agreed. “Good idea. We can blow it up, put him into a wheelchair, and cover it with a blanket. From a distance, it would probably pass as Har or Nick.”

“Let’s do that. Otherwise Vivian could make real trouble for us.”

Chapter 50

IMMEDIATELY AFTER BEN GOT back to California, but before school started, he finished the final draft of his cookbook and sent it to the agent who'd requested it. On the day school resumed, he handed in his resignation. He had offered to continue working until he could be replaced but would work no longer than the current school year.

After he did so, relief and anxiety filled him by turns, with relief only slightly more dominant. It wasn't that he'd miss his fellow teachers; they had avoided socializing with him when Cindy had become ill, apparently fearful that he'd distress them with information about his wife's condition. Mostly, it was the complete change of lifestyle that bothered him. He worried that he wouldn't be able to adapt, as much as he desired the change.

On the second weekend of the New Year he visited an old friend who was a building contractor, and they discussed the house he wanted to build in Oregon.

Jacques Silver had a slight build, but he was sinewy

with muscles and possessed a quick intelligence of *all* aspects involved in building.

"Before I get the permits, I need to know whether I should go with one or two stories," Ben said. "My property slopes, though not sharply. And I worry about earthquakes, though I know they aren't quite as prevalent there as in California."

Jacques nodded and scratched his chin, something he was prone to doing while he considered facts. "We probably *will* get the Big One pretty soon, and I'd build it with that in mind. One floor is always safer. The site isn't close to any faults, is it?"

"No, none are closer than eight miles. Do you want to come up and see it one of these weekends?"

"Tomorrow is open for me. My wife is driving down to help her sister in Santa Rosa; she just had her first baby."

• • •

Ben gave Jacques a rough floor plan of what he wanted, and then put the manor on the market, astounded at how much its value had increased over the few years he'd lived in it. He currently used only a small area of the house and planned to stay there until it was sold. Then he'd move into Rachel's cottage until the house was finished, even if he had to insulate it himself. Moving out would take little time and effort, since he planned to store most of the furniture. His books, which he began to box up immediately, would go with him.

His agent found a publisher, who wanted several changes that Ben didn't agree with, but his agent urged him to make them. "When you have a couple books under your belt, you can have more control," she said. "For now, just go along with all the changes except one; then they won't think you're a doormat."

So he did, although it was difficult to focus his energy on revising his manuscript when people were tromping through his house and asking questions he had to answer pleasantly. But he did manage to finish it.

• • •

His teaching career came to a close at the end of January, when a new teacher took his place. He left the school, barely hiding his jubilation. On the same day, Jacques called and told him he'd found a floor plan nearly identical to what he'd drawn. Building could begin as soon as the worst of the rains were over. Ben liked the plan and ordered the blueprints. The house was generous in size, since he'd need quarters for his wife and the live-in nurse she required. In spite of that, it wasn't ostentatious.

He went to visit Cindy more often than usual, telling her about the changes that he was making in their lives. He'd been told that she was probably unaware, but he told her anyway.

And then he e-mailed Rachel, telling her about his book, about quitting his job, but holding back the information about moving to Oregon. He wanted to tell her that in person.

He wasn't sure why.

Chapter 51

ONE MORNING IN EARLY February, Fed Ex delivered the inflatable man. Ruth was at work, and Rachel decided to wait until she got home before opening the package. She did, however, call her.

"Our package came. Why don't you stop here after work and have supper with me, and then we'll see what we can do with him."

"Sounds good. I get off at 2:30 today, so never mind supper."

While she waited for Ruth to arrive, Rachel sorted out the paperwork for her taxes, a tedious job she despised. Then she did some more quilting on the lap quilt she was making for Ruth. The ocean waves featured in the fabric dashed against a coast similar to the one in Crusty Beach, and the teal was identical to the shade in Ruth's plaid couch. Rachel felt certain that she'd like it.

When Ruth arrived, they went directly to the dining room, where Rachel had placed the package. She handed it to Ruth with a grin. "Be my guest."

Ruth tore it open and spread the vinyl man onto the table. "He looks a little too pink, wouldn't you say?"

"Yeah, and he seems a little short too. Well, let's blow him up and see if that doesn't improve his looks. Right now he reminds me of a boy I dated a few times in high school. Tucker something or other."

Try as they might, they could not force air into the vinyl doll. "I think there's supposed to be a little gadget that forces the valve open," said Ruth. "Like they have for some pool toys."

Rachel dumped the packing popcorn onto the table and pawed through it, pieces falling to the floor, but they found nothing. "An air compressor would probably work, but we left ours in Minnesota. Do you have one?"

"No. Let's take it to one of the gas stations in Crusty. They have air hoses outside. We probably shouldn't bring dear Tucker inside."

They jumped into Rachel's truck and drove to town, stopping at the closest gas station. They parked on the side of the building by the air hose. Tucker was soon inflated. There was a second valve for his penis, which they also inflated, just for fun. It gave him a thick organ eighteen inches long with a neon-orange head.

"Sons-a-bitch!"

They gaped at the doll until a bunch of giggling teen girls rounded the corner. Ruth grabbed Tucker by the penis and tossed him into the truck box, tossing her windbreaker on top of him. They took off down the main street of Crusty Beach, laughing uncontrollably.

Back at Rachel's, Ruth reached into the truck box, feeling for the doll. She stood on tip-toe and peered in.

"Oh great! Tucker flew the coop! He snitched my jacket too."

"That shithead! Let's retrace our route. He can't have gone far."

Rachel crept along while they both checked out yards, ditches, and parking lots. "Maybe he's straddling someone's mailbox; it'll be easy to pluck him off and run."

Ruth rubbed her face with both hands. "I do hope he isn't standing at the Methodist church; they are so down on nudity."

Outside of town a semi had driven into the ditch and was tilted at a precarious angle. The trailer blocked both lanes of traffic. There were two police cars parked nearby, but no ambulance. Rachel quickly turned onto a gravel road that headed toward the ocean and parked.

She said, "We'll park here and take a peek to see if he's in the ditch up there. It's starting to get dark, so we'll have to hurry," she said.

They scurried to a group of people standing behind the truck, while scanning the ditches for the fugitive.

A middle-aged man said, "I think the guy had too much speed or caffeine or something to keep alert and it made him hallucinate."

"He probably fell asleep and made up the entire story to get off the hook for the accident," a prudish-looking woman said. She swung her cane around. "He's lucky no one got hurt.I certainly don't see any naked men lying on the road."

In the grass-filled ditch, Ruth spotted the brilliant orange tip of Tucker's penis bobbing in the breeze.

Rachel said, "It's our property and we *can* legally retrieve it."

"You go first," said Ruth.

"How sweet of you," Rachel said, sarcasm fairly dripping from her voice. She took one tentative step toward Tucker.

The prudish woman slashed around in the ditch with her cane, bending aside some tall grass, and there was Tucker in all his glory. The woman let loose a piercing scream.

Everyone, including the cops, ran toward her to see what happened.

Everyone except Ruth and Rachel.

Slinking backward, trying to look invisible, they made it to the truck. Rachel crept down a gravel road nearly to the beach, where she took another gravel road that circled the town, and then took the long way home. "Do you suppose anyone got my license-plate number?" she asked.

"I think Tucker distracted them."

When they got to Rachel's, they stood outside in the twilight talking quietly.

"Now what?" Rachel asked. "Any ideas?"

"I'm thinking."

"Do you remember those big dolls they used to make out of pantyhose filled with polyester stuffing?" Rachel asked.

"No."

"Sure you do. They used them in store windows about fifteen years ago."

"Now that you mention it, I guess I have seen a few. They dressed them up and made them look quite realistic. I think I'll start working on one of them."

"Good idea. I don't think we could have gotten Tucker to stay in a wheelchair anyway," Ruth said.

"Nope. Too flighty," Rachel said.

"Indeed."

Chapter 52

VIVIAN SPENT THE RAINY morning stationed at her living room window, watching the road. As soon as Rachel drove out of her driveway, going toward Crusty Beach, she shoved her arms into her raincoat and raced over to her house. First, she rang the bell, then looked in all the windows. She didn't see Nick anywhere, not even in the bedroom, where the curtains were pulled open for a change. Then she tried the doors, which were all locked. She sat on the steps in the breezeway, waiting for Rachel to come home.

Nick hadn't been in the truck and he wasn't in the house, and she intended to find out where he was. She hadn't seen a trace of him for weeks, and she suspected that something evil was going on. Nick had been kind to her, giving her all that food from the greenhouse and even lending her fifty bucks. She hoped he would lend her some more.

She sat and watched it drizzle and soon became chilly, so she paced around the breezeway until she warmed up. She had to pee. Maybe she could step behind the garage. The rain began to come down harder, and she knew she'd get soaked if she stayed outside, so she pulled her hood up and stalked home, snatching her mail out of the box and also taking a letter addressed to Nick. She would have to catch Rachel at her house and force her way in. The letter gave her the perfect excuse. It was her day off and she didn't have a thing to do, or nothing she felt like doing anyway.

• • •

She woke up from a nap when Dusty came in from school. She made him two grilled cheese sandwiches, which he gobbled down while doing his homework.

"Thanks," he said, then brushed his teeth and left for work.

Vivian surface-cleaned the house, and then gave herself a pedicure, polishing her toenails chili pepper red. Every few minutes she glanced out her window, waiting for Rachel's truck to go by.

It was almost dark when she finally saw the lights on in Rachel's house, twinkling between branches of the trees thickly bordering her front yard. Carrying her faltering flashlight, she walked through the mist and stepped onto the wide front porch. She peeped through the dining room window but saw only furniture in the dimly lit room. She stepped to the door and rang the bell.

The entry lights came on, and Rachel opened the door. She didn't invite Vivian in but stood with one hand on the knob and the other on the frame.

Vivian whipped the envelope out of her pocket. “I just got my mail and found this letter for Nick in my box.” She held it close to her chest, making no movement to hand it over.

“Oh. Come in, then.” Rachel stepped back, pulling the door wide open. “Would you care for a cup of mint tea?”

Herbal teas gagged Vivian, but she handed Rachel the letter and said, “Thanks, I’d like some.” She hung her raincoat on the rack by the door, stepped out of her soggy clogs, and followed Rachel to the kitchen where she filled cups with tea and offered Vivian honey. She declined, thinking about the calories. They went into the homey nook, which was furnished as an office.

Rachel gestured to one of the chairs at the table where her computer was located. “I’m downloading some stuff and want to keep at it, or I’ll be up until midnight.”

“My son used to do all that, but then he got a car and a job. Now he hardly ever uses it. I ain’t got much time to use it myself.”

“Nick had to work with computers on his job, so he never uses them at home.”

Vivian glanced around the room and into the kitchen. There was no sign that the man had been in the house recently. “Does he still use his walker?

Rachel paused before answering. “Some. Usually he gets by with a cane.”

“Is he in watching TV?”

“No. He’s in the hospital in Portland having some tests.” She quickly turned back to the computer screen.

Why didn't she believe her? Something told Vivian that the woman was lying. "When does he get home? I need to talk to him."

"I don't know for certain. It depends on what the tests reveal. Most likely I'll pick him up in a day or two." Rachel stared at her. "What do you need to talk to him about?"

"I lent him a hundred bucks and I could really use it back." She held Rachel's gaze, but her nose began to itch so much she had to scratch it.

Rachel eyed her skeptically. "Funny, he didn't mention it to me. He can't hold a pencil easily, so I'll write you a check." She picked up her purse, which was on the floor beside her, and dug out her checkbook and pen. She wrote quickly, not even checking the balance. It must be nice.

Vivian took the check and left, determined to see Nick when he got back. Even if he could no longer speak, he could certainly dig into his wallet for cash. She was beginning to suspect that Rachel wasn't caring for her husband properly, and that she was hiding him from people. If she didn't actually *see* him the next time she visited, she was reporting it. It would serve Rachel right if she had a little misery in her luxurious life.

Chapter 53

RACHEL FELT CERTAIN THAT Vivian suspected something was wrong about Nick's situation, which was why she so readily wrote the check. The woman had asked about him several times, and it would only be a matter of time before she insisted on seeing him.

And then what?

It was too late to call Ruth, but she felt too jittery to sleep, so she pulled the dining room shades down and flung the newly purchased bags of polyester filling and the queen-sized pantyhose onto the table. She went right to work.

The bottom of the huge rag doll was easy, since she only had to fill the pantyhose with stuffing until it was as large as a man. The trunk and arms were merely a repeat of the process, with a few tucks and stitches to shape the shoulders. Then, she sewed the waistbands together and quit for the night. The hands and head required her brain to be fresh, and she was too tired to think properly. She glanced at the clock, startled to see that it was nearly midnight, so she turned off the lights and went to bed.

• • •

The next day Ruth came over to help with the doll. They weren't able to make the hands look realistic, so they planned to keep them covered. Unfortunately, they couldn't use that solution on the head, which they attempted three times.

"Except for his face, he looks pretty good, now that we have him dressed," Rachel said.

Ruth stuffed his foot into a shoe and tied it. "Yeah, he does look good. How about if we call him George?"

Rachel asked, "Any special reason why?"

"I knew a guy by that name, great body, but a face like a bowl of biscuit dough."

Rachel laughed. "George he is. You know those fright masks that kids wear for Halloween? The ones that look so realistic?

"Yeah."

"I'll bet we can find one that looks reasonably like Nick and Har on the Internet. If we add a beard, it would probably pass muster, unless someone took his pulse."

They went to the nook and found several companies that handled masks and ordered four over-the-head latex models, along with a couple of wigs and some beards.

Then they put George to bed in the guest room, carefully arranging his body so he faced the wall and covered him with a quilt. From the window, he looked quite realistic.

"You'd better get some curtains in here," Ruth said. "I've seen Vivian peeking through my windows a couple of times, so I imagine she does it here too."

"Yes, I'd better. But today, I'll settle for filling the bedside table with pill bottles and a water glass. I wish I hadn't written her that check, because I'm quite sure Nick hadn't borrowed money from her."

"I don't think she'll dare say he borrowed more."

They went into the dining room and threw the few scraps of polyester fill into the trash. Rachel said, "Let's grab a can of pop and walk down the hill to the neighbor's property. I want to check out those building stakes that I came across."

"Damn good thing we already did our logging."

"Would you like a sandwich first?"

"I can wait, unless you're really hungry."

"I'll wait."

They hiked down the hill stealthily, in case someone was at the building site, but they met no one. The day, although overcast, was nearly seventy, a treat after months of cool weather and rain.

Ruth paced off the marked area. "This is about eighty by a hundred, which is pretty big. They must have a lot of money."

"Or maybe a lot of kids."

"I hope it's someone who'll get Vivian's mind off you."

Rachel frowned. "What could she do? Report me?"

"Maybe. Anyway, I asked around and found out that they have some laws protecting vulnerable adults here. Maybe everywhere. They jump right to it the minute someone reports anything suspicious."

"Just my luck."

"I'm more worried about finding someone in time for those physical exams," Ruth said.

They crossed the property line and trudged back up the hill to Rachel's house.

"Maybe we could borrow somebody from one of the local nursing homes."

Ruth stopped in her tracks. "That might work. The one outside of town is called Crusty Haven." She snickered. "I wouldn't care to spend my twilight years in a place with that unfortunate name."

"Me neither." Rachel laughed and shook her head. "We could whip up a few lap quilts and say we were donating them from some woman's club."

"I only do the basics of sewing."

"They don't require much."

They discussed the idea further when they got into the house, thinking that it had possibilities. Rachel prepared sandwiches from rye bread with a filling of cream cheese mixed with a jar of slivered, dried beef, adding a spoonful of horseradish for fillip.

While they ate, they thrashed through possible solutions to the future problem of cashing in their husbands' life insurance policies.

"When the time comes, I suppose we could cruise the highways, looking for fatalities," Rachel suggested, clearly becoming desperate.

Ruth said, "Pretty slim pickin's."

"Or maybe we could kidnap guys from a nursing home. Ones who have no relatives and are on their last legs."

Ruth thought about it, smiling wryly. "We'd have to choose carefully. I certainly wouldn't want some forgetful old geezer around for ten years, pissing in my closets."

"Oh, yuk." She took another half sandwich from the plate. "Damn! This is a bigger problem than I thought it would be."

Chapter 54

THE FOLLOWING WEEK, ON one of her days off, Ruth picked up Rachel and they drove to Eugene to visit a nursing home. They hadn't yet made any quilts, so they simply walked in, pretending they were visiting a relative.

The residents were lively and involved in social and craft programs. Some were watching a movie and others were exercising. Even those in wheelchairs were animated and participating, not the passive individuals that Ruth had hoped to find.

They sidled along the corridors, attempting to find where the quieter residents were housed, but came across only empty rooms.

They crept down another hallway, where they found bed-ridden patients, all attached to IV's, sleeping, or, more likely, comatose. At the end of the hall was an exit door, through which they left. The cursed door tripped off a honking alarm that sounded like it belonged on a submarine, no doubt summoning some burly aides to capture a wizened escapee. They raced to Ruth's car without stopping.

"Damn!" Rachel said, catching her breath. "I was hoping to find a man in a wheelchair who'd *allow* me to wheel him out."

Ruth wiped the sweat from her forehead. "Me too, but most of the guys in there are so lively they'd wrestle you to the floor. And that alarm ..."

"No shit! We need someone like Har." Rachel slumped in the seat. "What nursing home was he in, anyway?"

"He was at that new veteran's home in Medford. They wheel the guys out onto the lawn for sunshine whenever it's warm enough."

"That sounds more like it," said Rachel. "I'll order a few yards of masculine-looking fabric for those lap quilts. We can sew them whenever it rains and we'll most likely have a few done by July." She started the car, left the parking lot, and headed for the street. "Come to think of it, they must have a fabric store in a town this size."

They found two, the first a boutique-type shop with high prices and limited stock, and most of that in shades of purple, lavender, and orchid. The second was huge, with aisle after aisle of fabrics for every conceivable purpose. They located the quilter's section, and after finding prints of men hunting and fishing, they wandered through the store, eventually coming back to the quilt-fabric section.

Ruth fingered some material splashed with realistic blue delphiniums. "This is so pretty; I'm tempted to try making a comforter and curtains for my bedroom. And it's half price."

"I'm no expert," said Rachel, "but I'd be glad to help you."

"Thanks! I have my grandma's treadle machine upstairs. I used to hem dish towels for her on it. I do a little patching now and then, but that's about it."

Ruth bought the fabric, backing, and batting, hoping she'd be up to the job. Sewing had never been her forte, but quilts and curtains were flat, square pieces. She'd likely be able to handle that, and if not, there was Rachel.

• • •

The next morning after breakfast, Ruth went upstairs to the spare bedroom. The old sewing machine was located in front of a window, where her aunt had placed it after she'd inherited it from *her* mother. Ruth's aunt had used the room mainly for storage, but had done a little sewing in here, too. At that time, the other upstairs bedroom had been reserved for guests, and eventually, Har slept there. The spacious bedrooms were divided by a full bathroom located at the top of the stairs.

She oiled the machine, squeezing the last drops from a dusty can she found in the machine drawer, and then filled the shuttle bobbins with thread for her project. To check the stitch length, she slipped an old shirt under the presser foot and lowered it. She worked the pedal, forgetting to start the machine moving with the balance wheel. She ended up sewing in reverse, creating a snarled mess of thread, which she cut off. She tried again and it worked perfectly. Because she was out of practice, the seam was a bit crooked, so she practiced some more, then repaired the hem on a sheet that had long been in her heaped-up mending basket. Feeling virtuous, she repaired all that needed to be done, throwing away Har's items.

She leaned back in her chair and clenched and unclenched her fingers to ease the stiffness from the unaccustomed exercise. For a moment, looking at her wrinkled hands against the black deck of the Singer, she had a sense of them belonging to her grandmother, who'd taught her to sew on a machine just like this. Where had time gone? It seemed as if it were only yesterday that Grandma patiently taught her how to hem dish towels made from carefully-hoarded feed sacks.

Ruth had never wanted children of her own, but now she felt a pang in her heart at not having granddaughters she could teach to sew, as her grandmother had done for her. She stopped sewing and stared out the window, glimpsing Rachel's garage roof through the branches. Thank God she had moved in. The similarity of their backgrounds made their friendship close, something she needed, and she felt that Rachel did too. She hated to think of anything happening to change things.

Vivian's face sprung to mind, and uneasiness washed over her. She sensed the woman's ruthless nature but could only guess to what lengths she would go.

Chapter 55

BEN STAYED AT THE cottage in early March. He needed to do some editing, which he found extremely difficult in his own house, large and quiet though it was. When he arrived at Rachel's, they chatted for a few minutes.

"I plan to do some book signings and eventually go on tour."

"You must have made a bundle from that book."

"No, I didn't get a very large advance, but my wife inherited a lot of money. I was only teaching to feed my ego. Now I'm writing, which is tougher than the hardest day I ever had at school."

"I hope five days are enough for you at the cottage. The electricians are rewiring it on day six. I gather that'll take a couple of days."

"That should be enough time to finish," he said. He went to the car for his laptop, a single suitcase, and a bag of groceries.

The cottage felt faintly warm, with none of the mustiness he'd expected to find in a building unheated through the damp winter months. He touched the Franklin stove top; it was a bit warmer than his hand. Rachel had lit a fire for his comfort. He scratched around the firebox with the poker, unearthed a few live embers, and added a piece of crumpled newspaper along with a few chunks of kindling and some wood. Soon, the fire was crackling, and he cracked open one of the doors to warm the cottage more quickly. After brewing a pot of coffee, he ate a peanut butter sandwich and got to work, making revisions until after midnight.

• • •

For the next two days, he barely looked out the window, not even showering or shaving. He checked his cell phone for messages but ignored all but one, which was from his agent. On the third morning, he worked for two hours, and the job was finished, except for printing a copy to keep.

He snapped to full consciousness, as if he'd woken from a deep sleep, amazed at the dirty dishes and empty food cans littering the table and counter. He had eaten, but he certainly hadn't cleaned up. Rachel would throw him out if she saw this mess. He shoved all the garbage into a bag, stacked the dishes in the sink to soak, and wiped off all the surfaces with a sponge. Then he showered and shaved and made a half-pound hamburger for an early supper, taking it along with a glass of milk into the porch.

The creek rushed toward the ocean, a white sound that at this time of year and in the winter blotted out all but the loudest noises. With about an hour of light left, he considered taking a walk, since he hadn't exercised for three days. But he was exhausted, both physically and mentally, so he went to bed and slumbered dreamlessly, with a rest that healed his achy neck muscles and nourished his depleted mind.

• • •

He jerked awake shivering, and listened to the rain pounding on the roof. After cranking up his electric space heater, he built a fire in the Franklin stove and brewed some coffee, taking a cup back to bed. He drank it and stretched, planning to stay in bed until the cottage was a little warmer before getting up to shower.

It was close to ten when he woke again. The sun shone through the windows and the building was toasty warm. Disoriented, he thought it was summer, but the fan on the heater reminded him it was early spring. He sprang out of bed and into the shower, not wishing to waste another minute of this sunny day.

His first stop was Rachel's. She was about to go grocery shopping and said, "Come along why don't you? I'll treat you to lunch at a new restaurant that specializes in seafood."

"What about Nick?"

"He's in Portland, having some tests."

"In that case, I'd be glad to come."

They had seafood platters, which included a heap of coleslaw. Everything was deep-fried, except the salad.

"I like stuff cooked like this," Ben said. "To hell with cholesterol!"

"That's for sure. Usually I eat food low in fat, but it always leaves me feeling oddly unsatisfied. Now I feel like I did when I was a kid." She grinned, leaning on her elbows lazily.

He smiled back and studied her face until she squirmed.

"I'm sorry for staring, but you look enough like my wife to be her sister." He took her picture from his billfold and handed it to her.

Rachel looked at it and jerked upright. "No shit!" She said it loudly enough for nearby patrons to glance their way, most of them trying to conceal little grins. She examined it carefully and said, "The only actual differences are that her face is rounder, and I think her eyes are a darker blue."

Ben said, "Yes, and her hair is a little reddish."

"I'd like to meet her. Ruth said that she's an invalid, but didn't know exactly ..."

"She has a brain tumor. She's supposedly unaware of what goes on around her, but I don't know. You can meet her when we move to Oregon."

"You're really moving here?"

"Yes. Perhaps by autumn we'll be here. This area seems to inspire my writing."

"Won't you miss your friends and associates?"

"No, not most of them. After Cindy went to the nursing home, people made an effort to invite me to parties. Occasionally women would show interest, which I deflected by telling them about her. Some people acted as though I should be sitting by her side rather that socializing, so I quit going and people stopped asking."

• • •

The next day, Ben packed up and left the cottage, dropping the keys off at Rachel's. He didn't leave the area immediately; instead he explored Crusty Beach to check on the current medical and dental facilities and other businesses. They would be adequate, he decided, for all their ordinary needs. There was a hospital in Gold Beach, which would do for moderately serious problems. Anything else would require a trip to Medford.

He wanted to live here and knew that he could get along quite well. And Cindy, well, it simply didn't matter to her where she lived.

Chapter 56

VIVIAN FINALLY CAUGHT A glimpse of Nick in March when she'd come to borrow some molasses. He was reclining on a new wicker sofa in the screened-in porch, covered with a pale pink blanket.

"Hi, Nick," she yelled to him, when she walked through the back yard with Rachel. They went into the kitchen.

"He doesn't respond to much of anything," Rachel said. "And he won't get better."

"I'm sorry to hear that," Vivian said. "I was hoping to ask him ..."

Rachel turned and glared at her so viciously that she didn't finish the sentence. She quickly searched through a few cabinets, slamming tall items aside. "It looks like I'm out of molasses. Maybe Ruth has some."

"I'll walk over and see. Thanks, anyway." Maybe the woman had PMS. She was certainly irritable.

She caught another glimpse of Nick when she walked to the front door. He lay motionless, staring toward the woods at the rear of the property. His face seemed a little thinner than it had been. Had Rachel been feeding him enough? Perhaps she should turn her in for starving the poor, helpless man. Then he'd be placed in a nursing home, something that would cost a bundle, and Rachel would lose her big, fancy house.

Vivian took the bridge over to Ruth's and knocked on the back door.

Ruth opened it, wearing a coat and carrying her purse.

"Would you happen to have a half-cup of molasses?" Vivian asked.

"Sorry, I used up the last of it at Christmas and I haven't replaced it." She locked the door and went down the steps.

"Isn't Har at home?" Vivian asked.

"Yes, he is. Why?"

"I wondered why you locked the door."

"I always keep the doors locked. Har and I got into the habit when the crime rate went up in Hibbing."

They reached Ruth's car. She opened the door and flung her purse onto the front seat.

"How is Har?"

"Fine."

"That's good."

Ruth sat in her car with an impassive expression on her face, but something told Vivian that the woman was pissed off. Maybe she was late for work. She turned the key and Vivian stepped back.

She waved with two fingers and followed the car out of the driveway. When Ruth was out of sight, Vivian swiped her newspaper out of the tube and took it home to search for a second job of *any* kind.

She was running late, so she tucked the paper under her bed pillow and left.

• • •

After a bitch of a shift at the café, Vivian trudged through the door of her sagging trailer. Her crabby boss had recently installed cameras in all areas of the restaurant and she could no longer supplement her groceries with freebies from work. With only two more support checks from her ex, she *had* to find a job.

Too tired to eat, she crawled into bed, taking a tall glass of ice water to sip on. The house felt chilly and damp, but she didn't dare turn the propane heat up because she needed the fuel for the cooking stove and the water heater. She burrowed under the covers and studied the want ads. Most of the jobs required advanced computer skills or medical training. The rest were unmistakably for younger people. One job was for a part-time housekeeper, the only one for which she was remotely qualified, so she circled it with an eyebrow pencil. Her greasy hair smelled nauseatingly like fried shrimp, but she was too tired to get up and shower. She turned off the light and fell asleep, having bad dreams about urgently needing to use a public toilet and finding all of them heaped with turds.

• • •

She slept late, not having seen Dusty, but finding his cereal bowl in the sink. Then she called for an appointment at the housekeeping number. A lady with a soft, sweet voice told her to come in two hours. Vivian showered, applied a touch of lipstick and curled her mousy, chin-length hair under. She climbed into her dull beige clothing and shuddered at her drab appearance in the mirror. She looked like she should be handing out religious tracts.

• • •

The new house was large, built on the outskirts of Crusty Beach. The landscaping, though immature, promised to be lush with azaleas in a few years.

Vivian hurried up the brick path and rang the bell at a set of double doors. The woman with the soft voice invited her into the foyer and led her through the first door on the right into an office.

"Sit down, Ms. Snell," she said, pointing to an ecru upholstered chair positioned in front of the desk. "I'm Angela Withers, and I am temporarily living here with my brother, Flint. He owns the place." She smiled widely.

Vivian smiled back. "The ad said the hours were flexible, which is good, because I work afternoons, but I can work any morning and all day on Sundays."

They discussed her previous jobs, and Angela said, "I'd like to give you a trial month. You can start on Sunday, when you'll meet Flint."

It was arranged. The salary for sixteen hours equaled what she earned for an entire week at the café. Also, cleaning that house should be a breeze, with only two adults living in it.

When Angela led her out of the office, Vivian picked up a small enameled ashtray shaped like a four-leaf clover and slipped it into her purse. She figured it would bring her good luck.

Chapter 57

RACHEL AND RUTH LEFT for their trip to Medford early in April. They stuffed six lap quilts into trash bags and packed them into the metal cargo box in the back of Rachel's truck. Luckily it wasn't raining, because their suitcases wouldn't fit behind their seats, so they were wedged alongside the box. After leaving Medford, they planned to explore the Willamette Valley, going all the way to the top of the state and coming home on the coast.

Rachel said, "I gather there are some fossil beds in the northeast part of the state. It's picturesque, if you like the high desert."

"Not especially. I see enough of that when I drive through to Minnesota every year."

"Good. I don't care for it either, but I thought I'd ask."

"This is a good time of year to travel before the tourists really start moving," Ruth said.

"Yeah, it is. Some year I'd like to poke around the upper half of California."

"Me too. Let's plan it for next year, about this time. Before the fire danger starts."

They stopped for lunch at a café advertising fresh bread baked daily. Dark, with several grains, they had the delicious bread with a peculiar soup consisting of cubed rutabagas and a handful of assorted herbs, with a preponderance of whole allspice.

"Most unusual," said Ruth. "I wonder what the ethnic origin of that soup is?"

"Maybe it's better that we don't know."

After a couple of wrong turns, they found the veteran's home. Ruth only vaguely remembered the location from when she and Harvey picked up Harlan for a visit.

They parked in the spacious lot, which was covered with dark, fresh blacktop. The building complex resembled several two and three-story Quonset huts attached at the corners. The grounds were lush with thick grass. Mature evergreens, which had been thoughtfully saved by the landscapers, were scattered over the grounds. Scores of young trees huddled in protective wire cages. Men sat on the numerous benches, some talking and some alone. A few occupied wheelchairs. Two attendants stood by the entrance of the main building, watching over their patients, while another sat behind the wheel of a car with the door open, smoking a cigarette with fast, deep drags.

Ruth walked up to one of the wheelchair bound men, and Rachel followed, carrying the lap quilts.

"Hi," Ruth said. "Do you remember a patient here named Harlan Lundahl?"The man said, "You bet.

He was always good for a light, before we had to quit smoking."

"He was my brother-in-law. We brought some lap quilts that we made in his memory. Any idea where we should bring them?"

"The reception desk would be the place to start."

Rachel handed Ruth half of the quilts and asked the man, "Are there any guys here like Har? Not speaking is what I mean."

Ruth whipped her head around, decidedly surprised at her abrupt question.

"No, though some of them gabble nonsense."

They left him and searched out the reception area, where they handed over the quilts to an indifferent clerk, who thanked them in a flat, unenthusiastic voice. They went back outside and visited with several more veterans, finding that there were no residents who fit the type of man they needed. Discouraged, they left. Rachel followed traffic signs to Interstate 5.

"I don't think we'd be able to kidnap any of those guys," Ruth said.

"No. They'd raise too much of a ruckus."

"Most of those guys in there look way too young. Not to mention way too dark."

"Yes. Even my cruddy doctor would notice if Nick suddenly developed a dusky skin tone."

"We're going to have to hire someone."

Rachel said, "Might be hard to find someone who won't blackmail us."

"Or turn us in for fraud."

They drove on, admiring the tree-covered mountains and the farms. They spent the first night in Corvalis and the second in Newport. They explored areas of the coast at leisure, stopping whenever it struck their fancy.

"I'm glad we took this little vacation. Harvey and I never got to explore the state and Harlan wasn't able to. It's no fun touring alone."

"That's for sure," Rachel said. "I haven't been much of anywhere since Nick died."

They were only a few miles from Crusty Beach when Ruth said, "Sons-a-bitch! We still haven't found anyone to impersonate our husbands!"

"I know. And we have only six months to find him."

• • •

Ben came back in the middle of April. He was working on his next book, tentatively titled, *Marvelous Recipes from Minnesota Women.*

"I'd like to have *any* of your recipes," Ben said.

"Okay. If you stay for supper, you'll be able to sample one of those famous Lutheran hot dishes. And this one doesn't contain any cream of mushroom soup or tuna."

Ben laughed. "I remember reading about those in one of Garrison Keillor's books."

Rachel grinned at him. "Mine is made of long spaghetti broken into inch-long pieces, shredded cabbage, crushed saltines and cheese."

Ben shuddered violently.

Rachel burst out laughing. "Now you *have* to stay for supper, just to taste it. It's grandma's recipe and it's actually delicious."

"It sounds disgusting."

They spoke of other things, catching up on minor gossip. Ben's hair had grown longer than she'd ever seen it, and it showed a lot of silver in his sideburns.

He noticed her gazing at it. "I had to keep it short for school, and I hated it. I think I'm taking after my mother. She grayed at her temples early, and the rest stayed brown for most of her life."

"It's very attractive," Rachel said. "It makes you look like a distinguished professor." It also added a few years to his looks and she thought he'd be a good substitute for Nick and Har, as all three men had similar coloring. She felt certain that he'd be sympathetic to their problem. But then she remembered his wife, knowing that he simply couldn't leave her and go running off to Minnesota with two female felons. She reluctantly put the idea aside.

Chapter 58

BEN ISOLATED HIMSELF IN the cottage for two weeks, trying out recipes from Rachel. He planned to use most of them in his next cookbook. The one made with cabbage and broken spaghetti would go there *and* into his personal recipe file. It was, as Rachel had assured him, delicious.

He visited Ruth and got a stack of recipes from her.

"Next you can go over and get some from Vivian," she teased, with a sly grin.

"Oh, no. She doesn't know I'm here yet and I hope to keep it that way for as long as possible. Besides, she's not from Minnesota."

Ruth poured tea and sat back down at her square kitchen table. "Tell me about this house you're having built. I'd love to see it during its construction, and I'm sure Rachel would too."

"It's not quite in the city limits of Crusty Beach, and you and Rachel will be our very first guests."

"I guess I'll have to satisfy myself with that."

He grinned and nodded. "How is Har doing? Is he still carving?"

"Uh, his knee pains him a lot unless he elevates his leg, so he spends most of his time upstairs. There's a television in the spare bedroom, and he likes to sit on the little balcony above the back porch."

"Don't the stairs bother him?"

"Not as much as the concrete floor in the garage. More tea?"

"No. I have to run into town to pick up milk and toilet paper. Then I'm going to the building site to see how the contractors are doing." He scooped up the recipes and thanked her, hoping he had enough for his manuscript. He'd already scribbled out the stories he planned as prefaces for each chapter. They'd taken him considerably longer than those in his first book, but they were decidedly more interesting, more polished.

• • •

At the grocery store in Crusty he literally ran into Vivian's cart with his.

"Why Ben, I didn't know you'd come here yet."

"Just visiting some relatives for the weekend. And how are you doing?" He pulled his cart away from hers and backed up a step.

A look of utter misery covered her face, and he thought she might start telling him the woes he didn't have time to hear. She might even fling herself onto his chest and cry. He pulled the cart close to his body for protection.

"So-so." She forced a smile and glanced at her watch. "But I'm gonna be late for work if I don't scoot."

"Oh. Next time, then," he said, hiding his relief. He didn't like or trust that woman, but he didn't want an enemy, so he always forced himself to be pleasant if somewhat distant.

He drove to his building site. The sheet of clear plastic that had covered the slab was gone. Piles of lumber and other building supplies were scattered around and covered by tarps. The overcast sky became suddenly darker, and it began to drizzle. Thunder, which was unusual in Crusty Beach, rumbled in the distance.

Ben glanced quickly around, hoping that by autumn this would actually be a home. He dashed to his car and left, grinning as he thought about how much he'd enjoy having Ruth and Rachel over to visit.

But not Vivian. Not ever Vivian.

Chapter 59

DUSTY FINISHED HIGH SCHOOL in May. He didn't, however, attend his graduation ceremony, asking that his diploma be sent to Corvallis, where he'd already rented a tiny apartment. His job started immediately, and he was working full-time until school started; after that he'd work part-time. Vivian gave him the support checks from April and May as a graduation present. She made enough cleaning Flint's house to live without them, although she had been tempted to give Dusty a cheap regulation watch instead.

On the morning that he packed the last of his possessions into his car, Vivian handed him a bag filled with no-bakes made with Rice Krispies, his favorite treat. He peeked into the bag and then grinned. "Thanks. I don't suppose you could send me some once in a while."

"They get stale pretty fast," she said. "I *did* put the recipe in the bag. They're easy to make."

"Okay." He looked around the yard slowly, his gaze coming to rest on his mother. He gave her a quick hug. "I better get a move on."

Vivian nodded, tears trickling down her cheeks.

"Aw, Ma, don't bawl. I'll try to make it back on Labor Day weekend."

She nodded and swallowed past the hard lump in her throat. Forcing herself to smile, she walked up the stairs to the trailer door and turned to wave him off. "Drive carefully."

"I will." He tooted, drove out the short driveway, and turned onto the road. When he was out of sight, she went inside and sat at the table, drinking the rest of her lukewarm coffee. She wiped the tears away, feeling lost and lonely. It was not likely that he'd make it back for Labor Day, not with the price of gas. Maybe Christmas.

She got up and poured herself another cup of coffee. It was normal for kids to leave, but the utter futility of spending seventeen years on the thankless job of raising a child hit her suddenly. *I did it all for nothing. And now I'm old.* She sobbed for ten solid minutes, feeling wasted, weak, and *ancient.* She'd missed a lot because she'd spent most of her time on parenting. Despite all her faults, she knew she'd been a pretty good mother. Now it was all over and she hadn't even been thanked.

"Sockcucker!" She threw her full cup of coffee at the door, and it splattered wildly but didn't break the cup. She threw a dish towel on top of the biggest puddle and pushed it around with her foot, something she'd never done and had chided Dusty for doing.

The tears threatened again, so she showered and got dressed to go to work at the Withers. She slipped on the expensive pink slacks and smock, paid for by her employer, but disliked by her. Pink was a color she truly loathed, especially this washed-out shade. She applied a little blush and some lip gloss, examining herself in the mirror. Her eyes were horrendously bloodshot, but she was out of eye drops, so she smeared a little gray shadow onto her lids to minimize the red.

When she picked up her purse from the couch, she noticed a bag full of too-small clothing that Dusty had placed there for her to get rid of. She'd add it to the pile of items for her next rummage sale, along with stuff she'd collected from the Wither's large house. She'd pick up a few more things when she went over to clean today if she had a chance.

• • •

The house was empty, so she let herself in with her key. She cleaned the kitchen, wiping down the cabinet doors and appliances. Then she started the dishwasher and mopped the floor. That finished, she cleaned out all four bathrooms, the job easily accomplished because the surfaces were new and needed only wiping down and not scouring. Finally, Vivian checked the office desk to see if any additional chores were requested, but no notes had been left.

After checking the time, she went upstairs, and then climbed up yet another flight of stairs to the attic. She'd been methodically searching through large plastic bins and wooden trunks for items she could sell at her rummage sale. Already, she'd dug through about a third of them, relieving her employer of what were clearly excess goods.

In a deep chest she found a pair of stained-glass lamps with dragonflies on them.

She went to the head of the stairs. “Hello!” she bellowed. “Anyone down there?”

There was no answer, so she carried the lamps downstairs one at a time and put them into her car. They were about three feet tall and the cords were old, but Vivian figured the buyer could always put new ones on them. She should be able to get between fifteen and twenty dollars for the pair, a bit more to add to her savings for the move to Las Vegas.

She felt so good that she gave the dining room an unrequested dusting and went home.

Because she was running late, she hauled the lamps in and dumped them on Dusty’s bed. She slopped together a cheese and mayo sandwich, which she ate in the car. Her pink uniform would get soiled with grease splotches at work, but she’d just soak it overnight. Besides, she had two more of the ugly things hanging in her closet.

She swallowed the last of her sandwich and hummed all the way to the café. The day, which had started out so miserably, had improved dramatically.

Chapter 60

DENISE, RACHEL'S OLDER DAUGHTER, called at the end of May. "Both Barb and I took a week of our vacations during the middle of August so we could come out and see you and Dad. Just the two of us—no boyfriends."

"Oh. Well. Yes. It'll be so good to see you. Do you plan on driving?"

"No. Even if we drove around the clock, it would eat up too much time."

"Well, good. Good. Do you mind sharing a room?"

"No, I guess not, but we'd kind of hoped that we could stay at the guesthouse. Then if we go to one of those beach concerts, we wouldn't wake you when we got home."

Rachel said, "I've already rented out the cottage until the end of October."

"Can't you kick the tenant out?"

Same old Denise, selfish as always. "No. I—*we* need the income."

They talked at length, Rachel automatically answering questions about places to see and clothing to wear in the cooler, damper climate. Her mind, however, was on the problem of Nick. He'd have to die and be cremated before they got here. Maybe next month. Maybe this week. But the fiction would be only for them. She needed the pension payments to continue for a while. The girls would certainly question her pink bedroom with the double bed, rather than the king-size one, so Nick had better die soon enough for her to supposedly make the changes.

Denise asked, "How is Dad, anyway?"

"Stable, but it's only a matter of time before he has to go into a nursing home. Home health care people can do only so much."

"Oh. I hope he's still home when we come for our visit so we can be a family again like we used to be."

"That ... would be nice."

• • •

The next morning, she drove into Crusty Beach for some groceries and stopped at an antique store that had just reopened for the tourist season. The owner, a woman in her 60's, was eager to help when Rachel requested something in which to keep her dog's ashes.

"Something with a cover. I'd like to keep it on the living room hearth," Rachel said.

"I have a couple of cookie jars," she said, steering her to the right shelf. One looked like a gingerbread man and the other like a cute little covered wagon.

"I think not," Rachel said. She scanned the shelves and found tea pots, canning jars, and brandy flasks, eventually discovering a covered jar. It appeared to be from the Victorian era, with fluting, a pearlized white finish, and a bouquet of dusty pink chrysanthemums painted on top. All edges, both actual and those created by the flowers, were gilded with rather thick lines of worn-down gold. She plucked it off the shelf and shuddered at the glut of decoration, but it was either that or a mason jar, since she didn't have time to search up and down the coast for urns.

"It's a slop jar, the surviving part of a toilet set manufactured in the later 1800s."

At least it wasn't a chamber pot.

After she put the groceries away, she cleaned out the fireplace and filled the slop jar with ashes and small-sized clinkers. Then she placed the urn on the mantel to wait for a private funeral service she'd have with her daughters. Even though he'd have to die soon, she would insist that they hold the ash-scattering ceremony in August, when they planned to visit. She'd tell the girls that Nick had requested a private, informal funeral.

Naturally, she would tell Ruth all about it. What Rachel most feared was her daughters running into Vivian while they were here. Or Ben.

What a twisted mess!

Maybe she could take the girls on a tour, going to Puget Sound, where she'd tell them that Nick wanted his ashes scattered. A lot depended on their reactions to his death. If they were grief-stricken, they could stay a night at a motel and then hurry back home. If not, they could spend some time together and see the sights, using up most of their time *away* from her house.

Thank God she knew so few people in the region.

Putting aside those troublesome thoughts, she picked up one that provided her with even more anxiety: *Who* could she get to substitute for Nick when he needed his checkup in September?

Further up the twisty trail of deception, *where* could she find a fresh body when she needed one?

And lastly, what should she do about Vivian? She'd been avoiding the woman, keeping the truck in the garage with the windows covered with newspaper so the woman couldn't tell if she was home or not. She kept the volume way down on the radio and purchased a pair of wireless headphones and used them when she watched television. The drapes were always drawn shut. The only time she went outside was during the hours that Vivian worked at the café, and she felt like a prisoner.

She would really like to tell the woman to go to hell, but dared not incite her, in case she turned Rachel in for endangerment of a vulnerable adult.

Then she'd lose everything, including her freedom.

Chapter 61

RUTH MET VIVIAN AT the mailbox, which had happened so often recently that she suspected the woman of staring out her window to see when Ruth walked down her driveway. She looked through her few pieces of mail while Vivian struggled to level her battered mailbox.

The sun gradually melted the foggy overcast sky, changing the June foliage from a dull gray-green into a cheery warm olive. It made her feel uplifted and even a bit friendlier toward Vivian.

"I'm having another yard sale in a week or two," she told Ruth. "I got some extra lamps and household stuff I'm getting rid of. And some of Dusty's old clothes. Do you mind if I park my car in your driveway on the day of the sale?"

"Go ahead. I'll keep my eyes open for it. How is your son doing?"

"He wrote me a one-page letter telling me about his jobs. He was bagging groceries for two stores, but he got promoted to clerking at one of them. He said his feet get sore."

Ruth smiled. “No girlfriends?”

“I don’t know when he’d have time. Maybe when he starts school.”

“And then he won’t mention her until he’s just about ready to get married. He’ll almost certainly spring her on you when you’ve got a migraine headache.”

Vivian laughed, mirthlessly. “I suppose.” She turned her face to the sun, shutting her eyes.

Ruth noted that numerous, fine wrinkles surrounded her eyes, even more than she had. The woman *had* lived a difficult life, and her hands looked a full decade older than the rest of her. *There, but for the grace of God* ... A wave of sympathy flashed over her, followed by a guilty gratitude that her own life had been easier.

“Are you sure that Rachel is taking proper care of Nick? My girlfriend at the clinic says she never brung him in.”

The sympathy evaporated. “She brings him to the clinic in Medford. They have more advanced treatment for people like Nick.”

“Oh. I still—“

“I’m certain that Rachel is doing an adequate job. Their daughters are coming for a visit soon and if anything’s amiss, I’m sure they’ll deal with it.” Ruth found it difficult to keep her tone friendly, but if the bitch reported Rachel, she could well lose a good friend.

“I suppose. I’d better get to work.”

Ruth unclenched her fists, not realizing she’d made them.

Vivian certainly had it in for Rachel, and she didn’t know if it was actual dislike of her or jealousy. It might be as simple as a personality clash. In any case, Vivian was capable of doing untold harm. Ruth didn't understand her motivation, though she frequently puzzled over the situation.

She strolled back to her house and tossed the mail onto the kitchen table, then left through the back door, needing a walk to dispel the negative mood Vivian had put her in. It also gave her a good excuse to snoop a little at the new house being constructed on the land below hers.

The walls were sheathed, and the steep roof was covered with deep-red metal roofing. Most of the windows were in place. Surprisingly, they weren't the huge sheets of glass so prevalent in many of the new houses, but moderate in size, with diamond-shaped, leaded panes. The owner had cut only a few trees and had hauled in almost no topsoil to smooth out the rough terrain. Either they were going to go with a natural setting, or they planned to landscape after the building was completed.

Ruth had just started back up the hill when a truck drove into the site and a husky, red-haired man stepped out and unlocked the rear door of the house. He'd been here twice before and was most likely the owner. She hadn't spoken to him yet and thought about turning back down to introduce herself, but she changed her mind. He might not like people skulking through the woods, and it was a brutally long walk if she had to take the road back home.

She had just neared the bridge when she met Ben coming back from getting his mail and she told him about the progress on the neighbor's house. "How is yours coming along?" she asked.

He smiled hugely, his eyes twinkling. "They've been working on the interior. I can't wait until you and Rachel can come over and see it."

"You *could* relent and let us see it before it's done, you know."

"I could but I won't. Not until it's done enough so you can get some idea of what it'll look like." He grinned again and took the trail to the cottage.

She glanced across the creek and saw Rachel hanging some exotic floral sheets out on her clothesline. "Is your coffee pot on?" she shouted.

"You bet it is."

They went into the screened porch with their cups and Ruth told her what Vivian had said.

Rachel said, "I have no idea why that woman dislikes me so much. Did you spend more time with her before I moved here? It's possible that she's jealous of our friendship."

"We never did anything more than have coffee together once a year or so ago. Most of our conversations took place at the mailboxes."

Rachel moved her surrogate husband onto one of the wicker chairs. "Sometimes that woman walks through the back yard, so I try to move George around a lot."

"Better throw that afghan on top of him, or Vivian will whine to me that you let the poor guy get too cold. What an asshole!" She threw her hands upward in exasperation. "Speaking of which, I have a cousin who lost his job when one of the mines closed and he might be glad to have a free checkup and a little extra money this September."

"We'd have to come up with a good reason why our husbands couldn't go for their physicals."

Ruth said, "I thought we could tell him they won a coveted hunting trip to Montana. For elk."

"That might work. For this year, anyway. Is there any chance that he might ask for a little more spending money when he wants something?"

"Um, yeah, which is why I remembered him when I spoke of assholes."

"Let's keep him in mind, but only as a last resort."

"Yes, let's."

Chapter 62

VIVIAN NEEDED AN EXTRA three hundred dollars to pay for the 13-year-old Taurus her boss was selling.

"I'll hold it for you till Thursday," he said.

Her rummage sale was on Friday, but her boss wouldn't wait even one more day. Vivian did have enough in her savings account, but she refused to touch it, having put it aside for her first month's rent in Las Vegas. To get there, though, she must have that car.

She walked to Rachel's, where she found her perched on a stepladder, washing her dining room windows. She reeled a length of paper toweling off a roll and crumpled it into a ball.

"I need a favor," Vivian said. "I wonder if you and Nick can lend me three hundred bucks—just till Friday?"

Rachel picked up the squirt bottle, and said, "We're a little short ourselves."

"I can pay you back on Friday, right after my rummage sale."

Rachel gazed down, like a judge in a courtroom.

"It's for a car my boss is selling. I need it so I can move to Nevada."

"Are you moving soon?"

"Before fall, if things go okay."

Rachel weighted the paper towels down with the bottle and climbed down the ladder. "I'll have to deposit it in the bank before closing time on Friday. Nick will be out of his medication on Saturday, and it's expensive."

"Sure." She followed Rachel into the entry, where she removed her checkbook from her jacket, which hung on the rack. Nick was sitting in the screened porch, his walker beside him. "He looks like he lost more weight," she said. "Maybe I should ask the county nurse to look in on him for you."

"He's fine," Rachel said, but her hand seemed a little shaky when she signed the check.

Vivian plucked it away from her. "Thanks." She sped into Crusty Beach to get the car.

• • •

Vivian held her yard sale on Friday. Her friend, Jill, went in with her, since she had several bags of clothing she wished to get rid of. They set up borrowed card tables in the front yard, hauled all the merchandise outside and pounded the sign into the ground. Then they sat down to wait.

Only two customers stopped by during the first hour, so Vivian went inside to use the bathroom, leaving Jill to take care of any customers. When she got back outside, she was delighted to discover that someone had bought the two lamps. People soon began to arrive in a steady stream, pawing through the items.

Only a handful of people were there when Vivian had to use the bathroom again.

Jill looked at her strangely.

"I have the trots, from all those fresh strawberries I ate yesterday at work," she whispered.

"Serves you right for being such a pig. I had to tell the boss that there was a lot of spoilage to cover for you."

"I'm paying for it now," she said, scooting back into the house and speeding to the bathroom. The high window, which was on the side of the house where the sale was being held, was still cranked open for air from the last time she'd been in here. She wasn't about to shut it now, since it was interesting to listen to the comments of the customers.

Oddly enough, she was certain that she heard her boss, Flint Withers, speaking to another man. She finished her job, but only put the lid down, not flushing the toilet. What Flint was saying terrified her.

"This silver trinket box came from my house," he said. Here's my name inscribed on the bottom. I'm missing several other items and some of them are here."

Vivian stood on the toilet tank to discover Flint talking to one of the town cops. Terror filled her and she stood paralyzed, wondering what to do.

Jill was asked a question that Vivian couldn't hear, but she did hear her answer, "I don't know who bought the lamps. They paid cash."

"How much?" Flint asked.

"Twenty bucks for the pair."

"NO! They're antique Tiffany lamps. Their value is nearly a quarter of a million dollars each!"

Vivian got down, feeling almost too ill to breathe. She'd damn near given the lamps away. They would have supplied her with enough money to live out the rest of her life in comfort, if she'd only known their value and found a dealer who wasn't fussy about checking on ownership.

Now, she could actually go to prison for decades.

She left the bathroom and thrust some clothing into a garbage bag and filled another with her photo album, all her important papers, her make-up and her new Teflon skillet. Then she walked out the door facing the back of her lot. With her heart pounding like a jackhammer, she crept along the creek bank to Ruth's driveway for her car.

She flung the garbage bags into the back seat and got into the front, filled with acute regret that she couldn't stay and milk some more money off Rachel. She drove by her own driveway, expecting to hear sirens, but she escaped, stopping at the bank where she withdrew every cent.

As soon as she got to Sacramento, she sold the diamond she wore on her finger, another bonus from Flint's house. While there, she wrote Dusty a card, giving him the bare bones of the story and told him not to worry. She'd get in touch with him when things quieted down.

She headed south, hoping that her newer car would get her to Las Vegas. The oil light came on after three hours, and Vivian dumped in a quart of oil. Another hour passed before it demanded another quart, but it was seemingly satisfied after that.

When she stopped for the night near Fresno, she didn't dare sleep at a motel, since she'd have to show her license, which could be fatal to her escape plan. Early in the morning she peed behind her car, then cruised the parking lots of Fresno until she found a car identical to hers. She swiped the plates and screwed them onto her car, burying hers in a dumpster under some rotting fast-food leftovers.

And then she headed east to the casinos, certain she'd find the rich man of her dreams.

Chapter 63

RACHEL CALLED RUTH AS soon as she came back from Vivian's sale. "Another woman is selling stuff there too, and she has some nice-looking tops in your colors. I bought two gorgeous lamps with stained glass shades."

"I'll run over as soon as I take the cookies out of the oven. Peanut butter."

"Yummy."

"I'll bring some over when I get back from the sale."

"Keep your ears open; I lent Vivian some money a few days ago so she could buy a car and move. I'd like to know if she actually bought one."

"She *did* park a different car in my driveway today, so that's true. I'm surprised you lent her the money."

"She made a veiled threat about reporting Nick to the county nurse. Is there such a thing here?"

"I'm not sure. Probably."

Rachel massaged her forehead with the heel of her hand and let out a sigh. "Things are getting out of control. I think it's time to find a corpse."

"Yes. I'll zip over to the sale and then come over. We'll figure something out."

"Don't forget the cookies."

Rachel hung up and replaced her bedside lamps with the stained glass ones. Then she went into the screened-in porch and adjusted the cover on George, making certain that the huge orange penis she'd sewn on him for a joke tented up the afghan. She grinned, imagining Ruth's reaction.

The day was too warm for coffee, so she brewed some black tea and put ii into the freezer to cool. While she waited for Ruth, she went into her bedroom to wash the lamps. Even though the cords looked old, they were in good condition, and she decided not to replace them. The bases were modeled to look like tree trunks, and the shades featured dragonflies flitting through a blue and green landscape. She turned them on briefly, and they glowed, contrasting wonderfully with the pinks in her room.

Leaving the old lamps on her bed, she went to the kitchen and added two full trays of ice cubes to the strong black tea. She was placing the newly water-filled trays into the freezer when Ruth knocked on the door in the breezeway.

She came in, clutching a sweater from the sale to her chest. "You'd better sit down," she said, looking both excited and disturbed.

"What is it?" Rachel asked. She sank down on one bar stool and motioned to Ruth to sit on the other.

"While I was paying for this sweater, the cops came there, along with a guy I assume is Vivian's boss—the one she cleans for. Anyway, the woman was selling a bunch of things she'd stolen from him. A silver box and other stuff. Also, two antique Tiffany lamps with dragonflies on them? They're worth about a quarter of a million bucks each."

"No shit!"

"And the lady who was working the till when they were sold has *no* idea who bought them. She said that unless she'd parked way up the road, she had walked to the sale. The cops are going around the neighboring houses, asking permission to look around."

"Oh, shit!"

"Last of all, Vivian shoved a couple of garbage bags filled with stuff into her car—she parked it at my house, if you recall. Then she drove away, and the cops didn't even look up."

Rachel's eyes glittered. "Now I don't have to worry about her spilling the beans about Nick. She has enough of her own problems. It's worth the money to be rid of her."

"She's sly enough to escape, I think. And the car she bought probably isn't in the system yet."

"Probably not. I was geared up for a confrontation with her. I feel a little let down."

"Me too. I was beginning to fantasize about ways she could die—by accident, of course."

Rachel laughed quietly. "When you come right down to it, she didn't want any more than we do. Just security." She stood up and got tall glasses from the cupboard and placed them on the counter. "Well, that solved one of our problems."

Ruth nodded. “Yes.”

“The cops aren’t getting those lamps! We could live on the proceeds from them for years. We have to hide them before they get here.”

“Where are they?”

“My bedroom.”

They scurried there and Rachel looked around wildly, then removed the pleated white shades from the old lamps and plopped them on top of the Tiffany shades, effectively hiding them.

“What about these ones?” Ruth asked, grabbing the old lamps.

“Put them in the trash pail in the garage.”

As they scurried through the dining room, they discovered a patrol car parked in the driveway. The doorbell rang simultaneously.

Ruth grabbed a lamp from Rachel and said, “Keep them at the door for a couple of minutes.”

Rachel did so, then led the pair of cops to the bedrooms, and bathrooms, stopping in the family room. “Please be quiet when you look into the porch; my invalid husband is resting there,” she murmured, wondering what they’d make of his erection. They gaped at George, then glanced at each other, dumbfounded. Rachel merely smiled politely. After they glanced into the empty living room, Rachel led them to the dining room.

Ruth sat at the table with one lamp beside her and the other on the other end of the table, with the appliqued quilt blocks and sewing accoutrements strewn in the center.

"No shades?" The younger cop asked. He took a casual look at the bottom of the lamp, where he no doubt read the Asian country of its manufacture.

"Oh, no, we need all the light we can get to sew these," Ruth said. She picked up a finished block and began a detailed description of the construction, using words such as warp, weft and funderbelt, further befuddling the cops.

After a quick look in the garage, they'd seen enough and left through the breezeway. Rachel stayed there, where she could hear what they said.

All she could make out was, "Minnesota women," which one said to the other, as if that explained it all.

"I really wish I knew what that meant," Ruth said from behind her.

"Yes. And what on earth is a funderbelt?"

"I made that up, just to confuse them."

They went back into the kitchen. Rachel dug out tall glasses for tea, then fetched the pitcher of tea from the fridge. She wheeled around abruptly.

"I have an idea. Oooh, do I have an idea! Let's buy a cheap boat and license it in Nick's name. In a couple years we can set it adrift in the ocean and say that Nick and Har went fishing and didn't come back. I think it takes seven years for someone to be declared legally dead, but we can live on the proceeds of those lamps while we wait for the life insurance. We would have a much easier time of things."

"Oh, that is a good idea! I ..."

There was a knock at the breezeway door. Both women jumped, still wired from the earlier events.

"Anybody home?" Ben shouted.

"Do you think he heard?" Rachel whispered.

"I hope not."

"Come on in." Rachel took another glass from the cupboard and filled them all with tea. She brought out a saucer of lemon slices from the refrigerator.

"Help yourself," she said, holding out the dish. "Let's take these into the family room."

She forgot that horny George was lounging in the screened-in porch. Rachel hurriedly indicated a chair for Ben to sit in, one that faced *into* the room.

Ruth glanced at her with a shit-eating grin on her face; clearly, she'd seen George's new feature.

Ben leaned back and said, "My house is finished enough to invite you over for a picnic-type of supper. My wife won't be coming until more is done on the place, but if you two would like to come tonight, it would be wonderful."

"Now that's something I've been looking forward to," Rachel said with a grin.

"Amen to that," Ruth said. "Where exactly is it located?"

Ben smirked. "Right down the hill. That entire acreage belongs to me."

Rachel felt as if she would faint, but she took a few deep breaths and glanced at Ruth, who was squirming in her chair, her face the color of bread dough. She asked bluntly, "Why did you go along with us when we cut down all your trees?"

Now it was Ben's turn to look discomfited. "Because I'm going to need your help with a little deception sometime in the near future. I thought it would give me a little leverage in acquiring it."

"He certainly pulled a fast one over on us, didn't he?" Rachel said to Ruth, giving her a wink.

She nodded. "Why didn't you just ask? We'd do a lot for you."

"Yes, we would," Rachel said.

Ben got up and paced around the room, but he didn't look into the porch. "What I want is a bit illegal. No, it's a lot illegal." He sat down on the very edge of his chair. "My wife is bedridden with a brain tumor. Actually, she's nearly a vegetable, but as long as she lives, which is certified by a visit from the estate lawyer once a year, her inheritance checks keep coming." He took a sip of his tea. "She has begun to fail and it won't be all that long ... And Rachel, you look a lot like her, and maybe you'd be willing to be a sort of double. And Ruth, you have experience in health care. I hope that maybe ... you can take over at the very end but not report her death. A new estate lawyer is taking over late this winter and he's never seen Cindy, just her picture."

The women glanced at each other.

Ruth said, her eyes twinkling, "Well, maybe."

"Please consider it," Ben said. "You know I'd do the same thing for you."

"Yes," Rachel said. She caught Ruth's eye and wickedly grinned. "We know you will."

Made in USA - Kendallville, IN
1094014_9780999368312
04.28.2020 1032